Steven Carroll was born in Melbourne and grew up in Glenroy. He went to La Trobe University and taught English in schools before playing in bands in the 1970s. After leaving the music scene he began work as a playwright and became a theatre critic. Now a full-time novelist and reviewer, he has twice been short-listed for the prestigious Miles Franklin Literary Award—the richest literary prize in Australia.

STEVEN CARROLL

TWILIGHT IN VENICE

MIRA®

*First published in Great Britain 2008
by Harlequin Mills & Boon Limited, Eton House,
18-24 Paradise Road, Richmond, Surrey TW9 1SR*

TWILIGHT IN VENICE © Steven Carroll 2008

The Love Song of J. Alfred Prufrock *by T.S. Eliot
taken from* Complete Poems and Plays *and reproduced
with the kind permission of Faber & Faber Ltd.*

ISBN: 978 0 7783 0229 2

58-0508

*Printed in Great Britain by
Clays Ltd, St Ives plc*

ACKNOWLEDGEMENTS

My thanks to the following for their help
during the writing of this novel.

My Venetian friends, especially
Geraldine Ludbrook and the late
Professor Bernard Hickey, formerly of
Lecce University. My thanks also to the Australia
Council for a six week residency in Venice in
1988, my introduction to the city;
and to Bronwyn Myers, former cellist with the
Darwin Symphony Orchestra.

To publisher Sarah Ritherdon and editor
Robyn Karney—many thanks. Thanks also to my
agent Sonia Land and all the gang at Sheil Land.

Finally, my thanks to Fiona Capp
for her constant help and suggestions—
and to Leo, the lion-hearted boy.

I have heard the mermaids sing, each to each.

I do not think they will sing for me.

* * *

We have lingered in the chambers of the sea
By sea-girls wreathed with seaweed red and brown
Till human voices wake us, and we drown.

The Love Song of J. Alfred Prufrock
T.S. Eliot

Prologue

ON AN oppressively hot summer day in a leafy Melbourne suburb, a thirteen-year-old girl sat slumped in a garden chair. The trees and shrubs in the deep garden drooped under the weight of the heat; even the vine that ran along the wrought-iron grille was barely holding on. The day, bored with its own density, had curled up under the green leaves of the garden and was waiting for night to fall. The birds, vocal in the morning, had given up. The house sat deep in its own silence. The wisteria, the flowering bougainvillea, clung motionless to the air.

Lucy, one leg draped across the arm of an old cane chair, was dribbling in her sleep: a girl in an old cane chair, a study in rest. Below, at the bottom of the hill, the river may very well have stopped too.

There was a groan, an ache, of a sound that became the saddest of music. It came out of the family stereo, through the opened French windows of the lounge room, through the mosquito wire and the decorative shutters, then poured into Lucy's ear. Slowly, she lifted her head, wiped her mouth, and turned towards the source of the sound.

It was one of those moments upon which a whole life turned, and which, when looked back upon in later years, acquired an air of unreality, but which unfolded quite naturally at the time. This music would be her life. Simple as that, not even her choice. This music, she was convinced then and in years to come, had sought her out; travelled across oceans, over fields and mountains, just to be with her. In the time it took for the music to pass from the lounge room to the verandah, she came to a decision. 'That,' she whispered to herself with a steely resolve beyond her years, 'that will be my life.' And when she looked back on that moment, years and years later, it would not amaze her.

And when she rose from the chair and her feet landed on the warm lawn, as she followed the trail of that music up the garden path and back into the house, there was a faintly registered sense of setting a vast mechanism in motion with herself one of its many moving parts. And, whatever it might be that she had set off, Lucy knew, with unshakeable adolescent certainty, that she would follow this thing through until it was done. For an event had taken place, and now something awaited her. But what? She wandered in from the garden, sleepwalking up the hallway of the house, following the music that had woken her, sure that if she followed it for long enough it would bring her face to face with that something.

PART ONE

Chapter One

Fortuny stood, in the crisp air of a bright winter's day, beside a low wall that bordered the street. To one side the river Arno flowed swiftly. The rain had been heavy across the northern part of the country the previous week and the water was high. He admired the clarity of the day, the castle on the hill upstream, the sun on the buildings across the river and on the trees that hid the many large houses of the city's bankers and the heirs of the Florentine merchants.

Retired musician, acclaimed cellist, his name for decades synonymous with the instrument and with playing at its finest, Fortuny was a distinguished figure, the most distinguished on the street. As a very young man he had once seen Ezra Pound crossing a large square in Venice, his distinctive black felt hat and his dark coat wrapped about him like a cape, as he had headed towards the Accademia. For an old man, the poet had carried himself with unmistakeable dignity, and Fortuny had raised his hat in brief salute, murmuring 'Maestro'—but not loud enough for Pound to hear. As he had replaced his hat, the poet had swept up the wooden bridge and across the canal.

Fortuny had resolved then that, when he reached a certain age, he too would wear a black felt hat, a dark, double-breasted coat that wrapped about him like a cape, and carry an ebony walking stick.

Now, at the age of sixty-two, he stood by the wall in his hat and coat—the stick not yet required. People passing on the footpath glanced at him, not only because of his clothes and distinguished air but because of his bearing. He looked noble, and indeed he was. Fortuny was not from Florence, but from Venice, and his aristocratic lineage could be traced back to the early days of the Doges.

His ancestors, a minor line that had entered the *Lista D'Oro* in the late fourteenth century after buying their nobility at the end of the wars with Genoa, had travelled as far as Cyprus in the service of the Republic. The name had always been the same, except that in the early days it had been spelt with an 'i' at the end—like, Fortuny was fond of saying, Foscari.

The family, before acquiring its noble status, had made its money from trade. They had been merchants. Peppers from Egypt, wines from Naxos, even cotton from Limassol. And over the centuries the family had served *La Serenissima* in various ways, but mostly in civil administration and trade; in Khania, Nicosia, Famagusta. It had often been dangerous work, so much so that when the Turks had finally conquered Cyprus, four family members had been lost in the space of one year. Two had been disembowelled in the street, one decapitated, and another flayed in the sunshine, his skin later stuffed with straw and the body paraded, headless, about the town. Fortuny still recalled his grandfather telling the story and, to his father's annoyance, laughing that the life of the modern public servant was never so colourful.

But the family survived. That occasion marked its most serious brush with extinction. After news of the deaths reached Venice, the only surviving son was dragged from his monastery and married; the union produced five sons and three daughters. In later life, his job done, he returned to the order of St Francis and later died in a small monastery on a hilltop overlooking Florence.

In time, the new shoots were once again directing the Republic's trade in the Aegean, the Adriatic and the Mediterranean, especially Corfu. There were whispers of Jewish blood, of curfews, of extended family members being forced to make their way back to the ghetto by nightfall.

But by the time the French converged on Venice, the Republic had fallen, was sold off to Austria, and the family was once again on the verge of bankruptcy. They refused state charity, adopted the French 'y' to the family name, and fell back on imports and exports. Over the years, the profits were siphoned into real estate so that, by the turn of the nineteenth century, the family members managed to survive and maintain the style of living they had come to regard as their birthright. And all from the spices, wines and cloth that had paid for their nobility in the first place.

It was Fortuny's grandfather, Eduardo, who broke the family tradition, having no feeling for trade in his marrow, his heart or his brain. He became, instead, a painter, studying at Le Havre, and later in Paris where he met the young Braque. In that year, 1900, he decided he had little talent for creating art, but a natural gift for recognising it. He returned to Venice, married, had a son, and set up a profitable business advising both the old and the new rich on the crucial matter of their artistic investments. And if an ancient family, with a sudden liquidity problem, needed to sell off part of its private collection, they were more than pleased to have an understanding figure to turn to, one who just happened to know that a gallery in Chicago was looking for a Ruysdael; a person who could guarantee that the whole matter would be conducted with absolute discretion.

Eduardo Fortuny was astute, with years of family wisdom in judging character and a keen, trained eye for the real thing. Very soon his fees were commensurate with the respect in which he was held, and the family never traded in peppers again.

But his son was impatient with the world of Old Masters, and sought to regain the power the family had once possessed. In the early 1930s—despite Eduardo's repeated advice to leave politics alone, that he had no talent for it—Fortuny's father, Vincenzo, joined the Fascists and eventually became something of a confidant to Mussolini. He entered government service as an amateur diplomat and took on the responsibility with a high seriousness that some found faintly comical. But he was as serious in this as he had always been about the family's history, for it was he who had first researched, then commissioned, the illuminated family tree that was currently stored in the study of the family house. He constantly looked back to the days when the family had had influence and power, and whenever his father was home it seemed to Fortuny that he was always mentally preoccupied. His lasting memory of his father was of a man who, like Il Duce himself, seemed vaguely delusional, with a faraway look in his eyes as if watching the last of the afternoon sun on a broken column.

When the Americans and British arrived late in 1943, the reprisals began immediately and Fortuny's father and mother were shot in the street a week after Mussolini had been strung up with piano wire by the partisans. His grandfather had died of a stroke in 1940. There were no other children, and Fortuny suddenly became the last of the line.

Now, here he stood in Florence, enduring a busy city intersection and waiting for the lights to change. He took his hat off and ran his fingers through his hair, which was always remarked upon as being silver, not grey. Fortuny was still a young man. He was consistently told it was a miracle, or that he had made a secret pact with the devil, for his face, his gestures, his bearing all bore the stamp of a young man. Even his sixty-first birthday party had become an occasion not to mark the passage of the years but to mark the triumph of Fortuny over time.

As he stood contemplating the clutter of the city, a young woman passed, dressed in the style of dark business suit that this generation of young women wore with a casual ease that he simultaneously admired and felt uneasy about. Something lost, something gained, he mused. When he thought of the women he had known, women of flesh and substance, he could never imagine them dressed like these young creatures. Neither would he ever want to. But there was something both alluring and alarming in the confidence of these young women, in the way they strode through the world—in the way that they implied they just might dismantle you even as they desired you—that was transfixing. As he contemplated this, his gaze rose to meet the young woman's eyes and he saw that she was staring directly back at him. Her eyes lingered upon him briefly, signalling pleasure at what she saw, and even suggesting in that split second that if ever time and the business of the world should conspire to bring them together then…who knows? She was, in short, giving him the eye, and there was even the hint of a smile, as she noted that the look had been registered, before she turned the corner and was gone. He nodded slowly, acknowledging to himself that it was nice to be noticed. Yes, nice, but unsettling. Why was that? He raised his head to the skies, contemplating the question.

The young man who had glimpsed the figure of Ezra Pound had also spent many hours immersed in the poetry of Mr T. S. Eliot (whom he admired much more, and whom he had had the privilege to meet once on tour). He was more than familiar with the lines that constituted the love song of Signor J. Alfred Prufrock. The signor, he recalled (not having read the poem for some time now), walked the sands of an unnamed beach, his trousers rolled up, seeking young mermaids, but also fully realising that he would be terrified if one should suddenly heed his call and emerge from the water wreathed in seaweed just for him. Ah… He addressed the corner the young woman had just vanished around: There is a touch of that in all of us, eh? *That* would be a poem, would it not? To say to the young man with the rolled-up trousers, Here, here is your mermaid. Now what? So while it was always a pleasure, and not an unusual one for Paolo Fortuny, when the eyes of these young creatures softened for a second as they rested upon him, and as much as he took satisfaction in seeing it happen, the confidence of these young women unnerved him and he couldn't help but wonder what on earth he would do if ever he came face to face, cheek to cheek, with one of them.

Just then the traffic lights changed. The acceleration of the motor scooters, the high-pitched noise of those tiny, overworked engines, intruded on Fortuny's thoughts, causing him to lift his arms and block his ears, but the traffic was relentless and at the next change of lights he crossed into a smaller street.

The street he chose was no quieter, and at one stage he was almost hit by a careless youth on a scooter who made no apology, provoking Fortuny to the point of pursuing the young scoundrel. He let it rest, but the noise, the fumes, the tiny lanes that were never built for buses or cars all combined to make his walk to the gallery an unpleasant one. Florence, he was at last convinced, was collapsing in on itself. Once, he reflected, it had been a city of flowers surrounded by green hills. Once, undoubtedly, a beautiful city, but now crumbling under the weight of an ugly century.

He determined that he would not visit here again. He had come for the *Birth of Venus* but the walk had upset his nerves. He now sat in front of the painting, trying to enter the stillness inside the frame. Always he had entered that stillness, that quiet beauty which had

resisted all the ugly centuries since its birth. But today
he couldn't. The sea-green of the water, the endless blue
sky, the hair that flowed to her thighs—thick, floating
on the air as if it were still submerged—and the gentle, undulating caps of the waves, the charmed green
wood… All failed to work their magic. First the walk,
now the tourists passing across his vision in their bus-
loads and the chatter of the guides made it impossible.
Fortuny was a man besotted with Venus, but the soft,
rounded form of the figure in the shell was constantly
being lost to him in the crowd. As he stood, violence
rose in Fortuny's throat. Standing a little over five feet
nine, he had never been a tall man, but he was impos-
ingly broad across the shoulders and chest, partly the
product of his genes, partly the result of a lifetime
playing the cello. Impatiently, he forced a path through
the crowd with his rolled newspaper. Nobody con-
tested his authority, his right to pass, and he made his
way back to face once again the ordeal of the streets.

That evening he rested in his room at a friend's house
on a hill, overlooking the river and removed from the
clatter and the noise. In the en-suite bathroom he took
pills for his liver and spa water for his skin and eyes.
At dinner he sipped from a single glass of wine and
picked at his plate before excusing himself and returning to his room.

His smooth-skinned features and alert eyes might

indicate a man to whom sleep came with a child's ease. But for a year now he had been waking in the dark, unable to return to sleep until the first signs of light lulled him into a fragile doze.

In the morning a taxi drove him to the railway station. Fortuny gave a last glance at the Church of Santa Sophia Novella opposite the taxi stand, before disappearing into the distasteful world of tabloid newspaper shops, where glossy magazines offered cheap pin-ups and tacky fashion shots of young men and women famous for—what was the phrase?—being famous. So this, he thought, this is the 1990s. This is the outcome of two world wars, of upheaval, revolution and mass death on a scale unprecedented in history. Is this what it was all for? This open-air prison of supermarkets and plastic shopping bags and piped music everywhere. Music, they call it! This is what it was all for? Damn it, he suddenly thought, give me war, revolution, anything but this.

In truth, since he had stopped performing, Fortuny's life had drifted from day to day. He'd lost the very thing by which he defined himself, and nothing—not love, or food, or drink, not even music— could any longer lift his spirits the way these pleasures once had. Fortuny felt worn out simply from the effort of living in this tired and ugly age, because he had lost the one thing that had allowed him to rise above it: the practice and expression of his art.

He waited for the train from Rome that would connect him once more with Venice. Fortuny, the last in
a line of ancestors that reached back to the Genoan
Wars, stood on the platform, smoking a cigarette and
oppressed by the thought that, in the end, it was his
fate to have become the full stop at the conclusion of
a golden era.

He adjusted his coat and lifted his Homburg, ran
his fingers through his silvery hair then replaced the
hat. His shoes were polished, his hat at the right angle.
The gesture, the manner just so. All was in readiness
for the journey. The age in which he lived may have
forgotten all decorum and grace, forgotten the proper
way to undertake a journey, but Fortuny hadn't. When
the train came, he would walk to his carriage over the
blown scraps of fast-food containers and discarded
newspaper pages of frantic, already forgotten stories.
Unhurried and calm, he would proceed: an emblem,
a living image of all that had been lost.

Chapter Two

EVERY night Fortuny performed the ritual of taking his pills, salts and water. No matter how youthful he might look, he had become obsessed with death. Every morning, he convinced himself, he could see the skull beneath the mask of his skin becoming clearer and clearer, and the bones, the body's framework, more in evidence than they had been the day before.

Not only was he obsessed with death, he was certain that he was soon going to die. The best medical advice told him that he wasn't, that he was as sound as a man ten, even twenty years younger, that he was imagining things, had simply grown morbid in retirement. But Fortuny didn't believe any of it. Every new ache, every new twinge in his head, his heart or his limbs convinced him that he was a dying man, about to leave this world a biological inadequate, who had failed to perpetuate the distinguished name that he bore.

Families, like empires, were prey to the same basic forces of life as anything else. They ran their cycles.

They rose, degenerated, fell, and eventually disappeared. Now his own name faced the indignity of oblivion. Yet for most of his life Fortuny had felt it could never end, as sure of his family's immortality as he had once been of his own. He placed the caps back on the jars he kept near the bed, drew the blinds, and lay awake in the dark until, eventually, sleep came.

The woman stands in a giant shell, at ease with her nakedness, as natural as the translucent blue waves lapping about her, as natural as the charmed green wood. There is a hint of a breeze, her hair floats in air as if still submerged in the waters from which she has just emerged. She is about to cross from one world to another, from myth to reality, her eyes direct, staring straight back at the viewer. It is a naturally ordered world, effortless, peaceful, silent. Arcadia.

But there is a sudden intrusion. Somebody is watching. A man in a black, felt hat and a dark coat, holding a rolled newspaper, is standing in front of the scene. Almost immediately a breeze ruffles the leaves on the branches, a bird is lifted by a current of wind, the sky begins to darken and the woman is suddenly alarmed as more and more leaves, scraps of rubbish and sheets of newspaper are blown into the air. Loud music, harsh and discordant, is heard, as well as traffic from a crowded street and shrill, crackling announcements telling this disturbed world that all trains

are cancelled. *Supresso, supresso, supresso*, the word repeated again and again over the public address system.
The wind now sweeps across the waters towards the
charmed wood like an oncoming disease, a plague
passing over the land, and it is the man in the hat and
coat, the man watching, who has brought this disturbance with him. Venus is no longer at ease in her nakedness. Venus is wearing a suit and eyeing the man
in the black felt hat in such a way as to suggest that if
time and circumstance were to conspire…well, who
knows?

The man runs his fingers through his hair: whole
sections fall to the floor, leaving him bald. Simultaneously, his face begins to sag about the jowls and his
body bends with the weight of his clothes. His eyes
take on the lost, vacant look of senility. There are harsh
traffic sounds and the figure droops. Street voices laugh
at the old man holding his hands to his ears…

When Fortuny woke his room was still in darkness. He
lay motionless for a moment, the dream still close, its
sounds only now beginning to fade. He touched his
hair, and although it was a cool night his forehead was
damp with perspiration. The bedside clock told him
it was just after three. Unable to sleep, he rose and hurried downstairs.

The back of the *piano nobile* was taken up with a
salon, where he had once held recitals, received guests,
and held elegant parties. It could be used as one large

room or, partitioned with heavy curtains and wall hangings, could become four or five smaller rooms. Fortuny himself had designed the wall hangings, and the fabrics had been woven and printed over forty years before by a small craft establishment on Giudecca.

The rococo ceiling, white with decorative gold borders, was dull in the night. The white walls were cluttered with paintings, over a hundred of them. As he emerged from the hall Fortuny hurriedly switched on a collection of lamps distributed throughout the salon. They had been especially designed by an artist friend to throw diffuse light onto the ceiling without creating glare.

Immediately visible were two or three minor sixteenth-century works and an early Flemish landscape. The rest of the salon was filled with portraits, nude studies, domestic scenes and rural prints, interspersed with paintings donated by wealthy friends and admirers over three decades.

Bumping into a chair in his haste, Fortuny made his way to the final, partitioned, section of the salon. It was a room completely filled with studies of female nudes, most of them painted by friends. Some were historical, representing seventeenth- and eighteenth-century styles, others were much more modern, depicting women from the 1930s, '40s and '50s—the periods clear not only in their hairstyles and fashions but also in the furniture on which they reclined.

But Fortuny wasn't interested in any of them. As he switched on the final lamp he walked hastily toward his favourite possession, positioned in the centre of the back wall: an exceptional copy of Botticelli's the *Birth of Venus*. Almost afraid to look up, but now standing where he had stood in his dream, he turned his eyes to the painting.

Yes. Venus stands in her shell at ease with her nakedness. Her hair lifts gently in the breeze, the translucent waves lap about her shell and the green wood remains charmed. It was, once more, a naturally ordered world. With a deep, exhausted sigh Fortuny brushed his hair back, touched his forehead and cheeks, then slumped into a small, padded armchair in front of the painting, admonishing himself for getting worked up about a bad dream. But much as he admonished himself (it was, of course, after three in the morning), one half of him was also inquiring of the other half if the dream didn't, in fact, mean something.

Outside, beyond the courtyard, the canals and lanes were silent. There were no cars, no scooters, no jeering voices in the street. The house was still, his servant, Rosa, was sleeping, and the silence worked like a balm on Fortuny, who stared at the work until he felt sufficiently restored to return to his room.

One by one, he switched the lamps off, their circles of light fading on the white and gold of the ceiling, as he made his way to the marble *portego*, a thoughtful figure receding with the light after his vigil.

He was alone. No, he thought, making a slight adjustment to the sentence, he was lonely. Fortuny, the great full stop at the end of a long and distinguished family line, was lonely. The salon, the doorway to which ran off the *portego* of the house, was over two hundred feet long, and as he passed through its various sections, staring at the paintings, the cello and piano, the wall hangings he had designed over forty years before, the furniture and the odd little inventions designed to chart the stars, it occurred to him that the only sound in the vast room was that of his shoes on the polished marble floor. No voices, no idle family chatter, no offspring. No need to separate squabbling grandchildren while entertaining their parents, no cries of outrage or musical bursts of laughter. Neither were there any lingering sounds of the parties, the post-concert receptions, lavish and long, that had once occupied the space. No, there was no residue, no gloss, no dust of former dialogues settled somewhere in the room. Fortuny, the great full stop, was alone.

But, he reminded himself, the Fortuny family had never been close anyway. The violent deaths of his parents (three anti-fascists, two Smith & Wessons, one Lüger) opposite the bombed remains of the central station in Milan had affected everybody about him far more than it had affected Fortuny himself. Of course, he never shown this or said as much. But the fact was that he had barely known his parents. His father, for as long as he could remember, had always been travelling. And when his mother hadn't been accompanying him, she had always, it seemed, been organising one fundraising charity occasion after another. Fortuny had been brought up by an Austrian nanny, for whom he had felt fondness, but nothing more.

No, the emotional and familial hub of Paolo Fortuny's early world was that part of the house in which his grandfather had lived. Eduardo Fortuny stoically endured his emphysema and spent his afternoons and evenings playing patience by his window. His grandson, who grew adept at giving the house staff and his nanny the slip, often smuggled the old man his forbidden cigarettes.

Throughout Paolo's childhood, it was Eduardo Fortuny who was the major influence on the boy's mind. He had retired, but the world of art he had brought with him, the paintings on the walls, the stories, the wonder of it all had entered the life and soul of the young Fortuny and never left him.

By the time he was thirteen he'd made up his mind, or, rather, as he later phrased it, his mind had been made up for him: his life would be the life of art. But the instrument of his calling was neither the paintbrush nor palate knife but the cello, and he spent many hours seated with it.

When the old man finally died, bequeathing Paolo a Flemish study of a music lesson, the boy wept to have lost his closest friend. And if, at that age, there was anything he felt compelled to carry on, it was Fortuny the Elder's dedication to art.

Just before the old man died, Fortuny performed part of the Elgar cello concerto in the room from which his grandfather rarely moved. Eduardo was seventy-seven, Paolo seventeen. It was one of the young man's first recitals, the old man's last.

The room, which smelt of death, of loose hanging skin and stale breath mingled with the scent of pressed rose petals, was lit with candles. It had been Paolo's idea. Seven candles (one for each decade), each in a silver holder, were distributed about the room, on the dresser, on two small tables and on the marble floor, from where they cast flickering rings of light.

Seven figures, in half-silhouette, were seated about the bed in a semi-circle, Paolo in the centre, his cello at his feet and, like everybody else, formally dressed for the occasion. His father and two former business associates of Eduardo's were in dinner suits, while his mother and a distant cousin wore evening dresses as if attending a formal salon recital. Even Eduardo Fortuny sat up in bed wearing a starched white dress shirt and bow tie. In one hand he held a large bubble glass of brandy, in the other a cigar. Looking at the fine Cuban weed, he laughed to the gathering.

'I should give these things up, eh? They're killing me.'

Fortuny played for eleven minutes and fifty-eight seconds. (His father liked to time his son's playing.) During the performance the room was still, like the blurred stillness of an after-image. Those present either closed their eyes or looked at the floor, or leaned back in their seats, idly gazing up at the ceiling as they took in the music, the room, the occasion. Fortuny the Elder drew on his cigar from time to time and sipped at his brandy, the music seeming to enter him like the alcohol, filling his veins.

As the last notes faded, the room passed into silence, disturbed only by the wheezing of the old man in the background. Silhouetted against the window, Fortuny's father wiped his eyes as his wife's hand reached out for his. There were sighs and silences in the room, and Paolo, exhausted from playing, leaned on the neck of his cello. It was Eduardo Fortuny himself who finally broke the silence, taking a large gulp of brandy and pointing to his grandson.

'Well,' he said with a smile, 'the little devil can play after all. And if that's not so,' he added, winking at his two former business associates, 'then I don't know the real thing.'

He applauded his grandson, his cigar clenched between his teeth, and light, respectful applause filled the room for a moment, while Fortuny sat, head bowed, his forehead touching the tuning keys.

The nurse entered the room, and one by one the

guests rose to take their leave and embraced the formally dressed figure of Eduardo Fortuny for what they sensed would be the last time. His lifetime business friends bowed as they left; Paolo's father once more wiped tears from his eyes, his mother dabbed at her nose with a white, lace handkerchief. Paolo, silent, drained, having offered the final, parting gift of his music, kissed his beloved grandfather on the forehead. The little group departed, leaving the old man to the care of his nurse, who was already removing the cigar from his mouth, the glass from his hand, even as they closed the door.

In the darkness of early next morning, the old man's heart gave in, the walls of its chambers fell to age, and the last of his living burst from his mouth like a broken steam pipe, gradually subsiding with a dying hiss.

Fortuny remembered vividly being called to his grandfather's room a little after four-thirty in the morning, remembered sitting beside the bed of the comatose old man, his doctor and nurse in attendance, while Fortuny the Elder passed from this life into family history. Death, the doctor noted, had visited the room at six fifty-four. And when the blinds were opened, an indifferent Wednesday morning light fell across the old bed.

For years after, whenever Fortuny passed the tobacconist's near the Accademia bridge where he had always bought the old man's cigarettes and, sometimes, the local lung-busters known as Toscanellis, he could see, smell and feel the past there, preserved in a special pocket of his memory. One day, when he walked by and noticed that the tobacconist's had gone, Fortuny, by now a celebrated young musician, could have wept all over again.

Fortuny learnt of his parents' death from a family friend on the afternoon of the crime. He went to his room, but he did not weep. At first he assumed he was simply too stunned, but as the days passed he realised that that part of him which would have wept had never grown. Throughout his twenty-two years, his parents had remained distant figures and in the end, perhaps monstrously, there was nothing to weep for. In public, he remained impassive, acknowledged the support of family friends, and simply got on with his life. His impassivity was mistaken for stoicism.

But there was, barely acknowledged by Fortuny himself, in some perverse chamber of his heart, a dull, sweet ache. The death of the old man had been natural, the cycle of life running its preordained course, but with the death of his parents in a blaze of some fifteen shots one rainy Milanese morning, Fortuny suddenly acquired a tragic past, which others would later read in his eyes and hear in his music, and which would lend his art a depth of lived experience that the others lacked. At such times as he acknowledged these thoughts, Fortuny could see his grandfather nodding and winking at him in approval. Take it boy, *use* it. It's not Old Father Time who decides what is art and what is not, it's people. And if that's not so, then I don't know the real thing.

Although many people had expected the tragedy to produce a major change in his life, there was none. He pursued his musical career with the same determination he had shown before the gruesome event, and in time he achieved the acclaim and the fame he'd always sought across all of Europe, as well as occasional engagements to perform in the United States.

Fame brought good and bad days, the exciting and the tedious, nothing more tedious than the many interviews he was forced to grant. One, in particular, always stuck in his mind A young journalist, who clearly thought he was talking to a pop guitarist or some such minstrel, asked him in all seriousness what he thought the colour of his music was. Colour? Fortuny, having never before (or since) seen his music in any colour, eyed the young fool, stared at the blue and green wallpaper of the hotel foyer in which they were sitting, and shrugged. Then, blues and greens, he'd said, contemptuous of the question. Music, he inwardly informed the young journalist, was colourless, odourless, etcetera, etcetera. Music is sound. For, as much as he was happy to be feted as an artist, he also prided himself, metaphorically speaking, on having his grandfather's feet, which were always firmly planted on the ground.

It had been a busy life, punctuated with love affairs—the most enduring with a surgeon's wife in Paris. But he had never married, and never become a father. Marriage and fatherhood always seemed to belong to the future, something other people did, something to be thought about when the next series of tours was completed. A perpetual option. Thus, the family line, from the Genoan Wars and the last, sweet breaths of the Most Serene Republic, had come down to Fortuny, now falling back into bed for a few brief hours before facing another day.

Chapter Three

IN THE morning, the hangover of his dream still with him, Fortuny rose early, determined to shrug off the night's melancholy by completing a long overdue purchase before attending a student recital at the Conservatorium. The first stop, always a pleasure, was a visit to the stationer, for Fortuny was, and always had been, a meticulous letter writer.

'Look, Don Paolo.' The shopkeeper smiled. 'Look at this paper. Feel it.'

The specialist stationery store had been established in 1743, changed its name to *L'Art d'Écrire* during the Napoleonic invasion, and left it at that. The current owner was in a direct family line from the shop's founder. The name on the sign at the front had not changed in all those years, neither would it when the next generation took over.

'And the colour,' said the owner. 'So rich.'

Fortuny could see the father's face in that of the current owner, and no doubt others would make exactly the same observation in the years to come. The shop, still in San Marco, was where Fortuny had always ordered his stationery, his writing paper, envelopes and cards. It was a family custom, initiated by his grandfather. The family insignia, a light blue crescent, was always in the left-hand corner of the paper, the paper itself always made to order.

The owner was now displaying a range of special-occasion cards.

'The print, Don Paolo,' he pointed out, 'is very clean.'

Fortuny picked up a card, smiling to himself as he examined its image of old Venice—the owner was the only person in Venice who called him 'Don'. To his students he was Maestro, to everybody else he was simply Fortuny, or Signor Fortuny. Never Don. And, although the family had always been untitled nobility, Fortuny concluded that the man's manner of address was more than simply good business practice. Cynicism might have led him to a different conclusion, but Fortuny detected a genuine deference and affection in the man's speech and gesture. And all of it, the titles, manners and rituals, implying those deep structures that quietly ran through society like the canals in the city, had become of increasing importance to Fortuny over recent years.

When Fortuny had stopped performing the previous year at the age of sixty-one, a vast, rolling emptiness had entered his life, what he could only call a shadow over the heart, and he had felt alone for the first time. The industry of his life had ground to a halt, and the cameraderie, the friendships, the associations of years had all gradually seemed to fade. And with the year that had passed, so the women had seemed to pass from his life as well. Nowadays he felt like a spectator of a sport that he had once played when he'd been a young man, but played no more. And when he didn't imagine himself like that, he was left wondering what to do with all the restless energy that he had once expended on art and love.

His last liaison had been with Sophia, a singer in her late thirties. He had taken her to a restaurant on the Giudecca and, as he had for all the affairs of his life, he had prepared his bedroom in readiness to receive her later: wine and glasses on a tray; chocolates; subtle lighting; an open window to allow in the sounds and night sky of the city outside. And when, later, she removed her garments and stood before him like all the women of his life till then, with the predictability, the regular rhythms of a ceremony, he ran his hands over her body like a blind man being led by touch. The girl was there, but where was the music, the adulation of applause, the rush the playing had always filled him with, and the need for release that always came with the utter concentration of performance? Where was the thrill, the sheer intensity of the ritual? The night had been a failure.

He had offered, as he always did on these occasions, to see her to the door, but she had politely refused. She had spoken out of consideration, but what she hadn't known was that it was part of Fortuny's custom. The invitation to dinner after the show, the lovemaking and the farewell. These observances were crucial, like the beginning, the middle and the end of a performance, only there had been no performance. Yet, if he could only see her to the door, then perhaps something of the evening might be salvaged. Yes, the details were important, making for a deeply satisfying continuity. So he would always guide his women through the house, as though its halls and rooms were as labyrinthine as the city outside and strangers not to be left to its many deceptions. It was both a responsibility and a pleasure. He would take them by the arm, lead them through the still, dark house, and take his farewell at the door that led down onto the walled courtyard, silver and shimmering under a night sky, its statues, plants, hanging boughs and departing lovers, all reminiscent of the fleeting stuff of dreams made real for a few, sweet moments.

He had listened to Sophia's steps in the *portego*, listened to the closing of doors. And then, looking from the window to the wooden bridge, he saw her in the still quiet of the early morning. Saw her bright, blue dress and even heard in the distance, unimpeded, carried through the clear air, the rapid clip of her shoes as she swept up the steps and onto the other side of the Accademia bridge.

He watched as she disappeared, then turned once more to face the scene that his room presented. In the past this was the moment when he would recline on his bed to inscribe the events of the evening into his bound diary. But not that night. On that night, Fortuny gathered the silver dish of chocolates, the glasses from which no wine had been drunk, and slowly, carefully, removed them from the room. The affairs, the pursuits, the long, lingering philandering life of 'Don' Paolo, it seemed, was over. And what did he have to show for all the years? Already, he had become yesterday's man.

After that night no woman returned to Fortuny's room, and without intending it his life became increasingly solitary. Whereas he had once thought nothing of asking a woman to dine with him, he now walked the Lido at sunset alone, his trousers rolled up, half wishing, half dreading the call of those fabled creatures out there beneath the dark waves and the wreaths of swaying seaweed.

Over those aimless months, in which his life drifted like an impromptu exercise that showed no sign of closure, the emptiness he felt was gradually filled with a dutiful sense of family history, and the Old Europe from which it had sprung. It was as though, at a deeply significant social level, he was indebted to the order that had produced and nurtured him, and which he had rewarded by squandering his progenitor's seed throughout the bedrooms of Europe. And to demonstrate his new-found sense of duty, he renovated the family house, restored the paintings, redecorated the impressive ceilings. Gradually he came to observe certain historical occasions and donated generously to the appropriate institutions and organisations. And if he could lend the substance of his name and artistic reputation to the right societies, he did…

'There, Don Paolo.' The shopkeeper handed the small parcel of paper and envelopes over the counter. Outside, the parcel under his arm, he followed a small lane and mingled with the commerce of the street, his hat, coat and bearing distinctively that of Fortuny.

The music school was only a short walk away. As Fortuny approached the Conservatorium, students whom he passed nodded their greetings, addressing him with the title he had become accustomed to over the years: Maestro.

He had always kept in touch with the academy and was still often asked to listen to the students' work, even though he dropped in less and less these days. As he passed the practice rooms he caught the intermittent sounds of pianos, violins, cellos and, near the front of the building, a percussionist playing the same phrase over and over again. He normally found this pastiche of sounds pleasing, but this morning it was an irritating jumble.

In the recital room he was to listen to four new students—cello, piano and violin. Fortuny knew that after each piece they would, as usual, look nervously in the direction of the Maestro, who would either nod or remain impassive depending on the quality of the playing. His response, or lack of it, would immediately be translated into a definitive judgement by the students, who would take account of the slightest emphasis, even the manner of a nod.

For most of the morning in the recital room Fortuny looked down at the marble floor, listening to indifferent renditions of the usual recital favourites. His mind was still restless from the previous night's poor sleep, still brooding over thoughts that always arose in the early hours of the morning and which were best left in the early hours of the morning, when he was suddenly stopped by a sensation like a small wave passing through him. It was a sensation both distant and familiar, and drew him back from the fragments of the uneasy, broken dreams his tired mind had washed up for contemplation. It was, in fact, a sharp, rasping couple of notes on the cello, followed by a smooth, melodic progression, smooth as the drifting deep sleep of a healthy body. Furthermore, he could visualise at will the black and white notations of the suite he had played all his life. It was a deceptively difficult piece, not a student favourite, but whenever it was played it was invariably rushed or indulgently florid. But there, in front of him, it seemed to be performed without nerves, fresh and confident as though the student, protected by her youth, had never been told of the difficulty of the piece. And in those first few seconds of listening he even smiled, hoping nobody would notice—not just yet—in case she realised she was flying after all and happened to look down.

She was the last of the new students. Fortuny listened, watched and, in the process, completely forgot the disturbances of the previous night as the music, its deep notes and chords, like the distant moan of the Adriatic ferries departing in the evening, took him over.

He noticed that the student was a tall young woman, probably in her early twenties, and that she played with a strong, straight back, her feet planted firmly on the floor either side of the instrument, like a tradesman. But while Fortuny had been staring at the floor, lost in his own thoughts, he had missed her introduction and not caught the name of this new arrival.

Not that it mattered. He rarely stayed around afterwards and rarely met the students. And so, as was his custom, when the young woman had finished and the recital was over, he rose and swiftly manoeuvred his way to the exit and departed. But the music followed him, and that sensation of his heart suddenly lifting with those rolling waves of sound, went with him out into the courtyard.

PART TWO

Chapter Four

THE walk to the stage was the longest of her life. Lucy McBride and her fellow students were seated in a row along the far wall near the front. When her time came she rose from the canvas chair and walked the few metres to where her cello waited for her. As she walked, the sunny canal outside appearing inviting through the window, she made the mistake of looking upwards. The painted blue sky of the ceiling was suddenly vaster, more immense than it had seemed a week before, the stage itself wider and more imposing, the makeshift wooden steps leading to it creaking in the hush as she ascended.

Since being roused in the garden that afternoon ten years before by the music she was about to perform, her life had been directed towards just such a moment. The music, she had learnt from her parents, was Bach, the cellist a certain Paolo Fortuny. From that day on the two merged: Bach and Fortuny. She would not only play that music but one day she would play it just like the Maestro himself, whose playing had roused her from her childhood. In many ways, that long-ago summer's day had been the day her childhood had ended.

Lucy was an only child and her parents—father a doctor, mother a teacher—recognised the passion that fired her. They bought her the best cello, and she did not let them down. From then on everything, beginning with the buying of the cello, the practising, day and night, the reading, the attentive listening, the concerts and recitals she attended either with her parents or her select group of friends at the Methodist Ladies College (Helena Applegate, whose legs were famous, and Sally Happer, who kept a journal), even her chosen foreign language, Italian: everything was directed towards just such a moment as this.

The distant, famous figure of Fortuny became a constant presence in her life over the years, to the extent that she came, in time, to feel as though she knew him. To call it a crush was to demean the substance and sheer force of what she felt. Neither was it a mere daydream, a plaything to be dragged out and toyed with at idle moments. The music and Fortuny, his life and hers, were integral parts of a dream so grand, so epic, the most enchanting of myths, that she dare not speak of it to anyone. But it didn't become an ache, a physical sensation, until she wandered into one of the main music stores in the city one Saturday morning.

Inside the still, separate world of that shop, Lucy had

stood for a moment near the doorway, listening to the whispered conversation between a customer and the shop owner, and hearing the brittle sound of old pages being turned on the counter beside her. She slowly drifted towards the record shelves, her feet knowing the way, and in the quiet that surrounded her, like the quiet of a library or a church, began idly flicking through the recordings.

It was then, while she was registering the names on the records—Bach, Beethoven, Brahms—that she saw Fortuny for the first time. The first three record albums she'd had, pastoral scenes adorning the covers, had come without photographs of the artist and supplied only the barest biographical details. But on that morning she discovered a recording of Fortuny's with a large black and white photograph of him on the back of the sleeve. Until then, she'd known only the music. She stood still, stunned, staring at the cover, checking the name, once, twice. Making sure.

Strange, never to have seen him before. The photograph had been taken by Man Ray in a Rome studio in 1962. It showed a young, pensive Fortuny, his hair swept back, his dark eyes sad (she had read somewhere about the tragic fate of his parents), with a slight studio shadow across one side of his face. He was impeccably dressed in what she already recognised was a cut of clothing above anything she normally saw. The thought that Fortuny might be handsome or, in the manner of a film star, glamorous had never occurred to Lucy. In her mind he'd always been somehow unreachable, like God. But there, in front of her, was the evidence of a real man. Paolo Fortuny was the complete, sophisticated, European gentleman. The kind to whom everything—art, women, small talk, lighting a cigarette—came with effortless ease, the kind who always knew precisely what was required at precisely the right time, the kind that lived on only in books and films (and old ones at that). Or did they?

Fortuny's music had long since entered Lucy's life, but on that day she felt an unmistakeable ache enter her, just beneath the heart, like a short sword between her seventh and eighth ribs. An impossible love, which made the ache all the more exquisite. She had fallen in love with Fortuny's music, but staring at the portrait that afternoon she fell in love with Fortuny the maker of the music, Fortuny the man, Fortuny's world. Above all, she fell in love with the idea of Fortuny, with an image redolent of worlds far removed from her own. She lifted the recording from the stack and walked towards the counter with the cover pressed to her chest like some illicit, pornographic novel.

On the street, in the bus, everybody stared. Everybody. And it wasn't her imagination. As if the symptoms of love, like pregnancy, were clear to the practised eye, to all those who knew what the condition felt and looked like. And if the talk of the school locker rooms and dormitories had in the past been a source of annoyance, now it was an irrelevance.

She thought of pinning the photograph to her wall but then it would be on display, and her parents, school friends and visitors, anybody, would notice and ask questions. In the end she told no one, and Fortuny became a secret, unspoken passion. The quiet, thrilling secret she carried through adolescence. In the following weeks she visited music libraries, general libraries, and sought out articles on Fortuny, reviews of his work. She even found a book, a biography printed in the late 1970s. She read all about his life, his aristocratic lineage, the details surrounding the tragic deaths of his parents, his concerts, his travels, his love affairs. And there were more photographs. Fortuny at work or with friends; Fortuny a little older, but no less impressive. And his house, a small palazzo in fact, was photographed twice. Once, as seen from the Grand Canal which it faced, with its colourful, tall, Arabian arches. Another shot, interior, showed a large salon, its walls cluttered with paintings, the floor arranged with small sculptures, embroidered cloths—designed by Fortuny—hanging from the walls, lamps designed by Fortuny on the briarwood tables, and the man himself, sitting in an old armchair beside his cello. A woman, his long-time servant, her hair pulled severely back, stood in the background, a silver tray in her hands. So, this was Fortuny's world.

From that moment on, whenever she played, she played for Fortuny. He was there, watching, observing, commenting. Nodding approvingly at certain moments in her performance, shaking his head at others. There were even moments of conversation, but only moments. For Lucy found it difficult to imagine the sound of Fortuny's voice, the words, the observations, the flow of the sentences. There were only the photographs. His voice, the sounds of his life remained a mystery. Their imagined communications were either simply understood, like those of a dream, or were the words she'd read in the music magazines to which Fortuny had given interviews.

In this way, during the months that followed, understandings were established and Lucy gradually came to know Fortuny. She had always seen his music in terms of greens and blues. Not like a harsh summer sky, glaring and impossible, but dark and brooding. Then, when she read one day in a classical music magazine that these were indeed the colours in which he saw his music, the truth of her instincts was confirmed. He had even added that he trusted the logic of his instincts above all other responses, and Lucy could only nod as she read the article, pronouncing the word 'Yes' and again, 'Yes'.

Whenever she thought of him, she inevitably thought of that photograph, one of a series shot during a hot and ill-tempered summer morning in Rome, over twenty years before she was born.

In her room, as well as the photographs of Fortuny, spread over her bed, the floor and her desk were maps and guide books of Venice, Fortuny's city. She studied them endlessly and knew the main thoroughfares, streets and squares as well as she knew any city on earth. Perhaps better than any city on earth.

Often, she idly ran her index finger over the course of the Grand Canal, lingering at the churches and palazzos that lined its way. Then she would trace the network of twisting lanes that ran from the station down to the Rialto, and on to the Piazza San Marco. And, inevitably, of its own accord, her finger always followed the numerous streets and entered the many squares that lay beyond San Marco, tripping lightly over the Accademia bridge, till it eventually came to the Ca' Fortuny.

There, the languid finger of Lucy McBride always paused, slowly circling the spot. Sometimes she even dozed at night surrounded by the maps of her imagined city. A city she knew as well as a mathematician knew a distant star. All that remained now was to step into it.

And so she did. Lucy had already lived in Cambridge for a year as child when her mother had taught at a private school just outside Huntingdon. During that year, she and her parents would take off on weekends and school holidays, stopping in Paris (always staying at the best places) and haunting every gallery in the city or driving through the French and Italian countryside. But they'd never seen Venice. Now, at the end of Lucy's fifth year at school, when her parents (keen travellers in their childless youth) took her on her second trip to Europe, the high point of this trip was a week at the Gritti Palace in Venice. They always did that, her parents. Stayed at the best. Not that they could really afford the best, but the licence to do so, in fact, the imperative that one *must* do so, was somehow written into the family.

Her mother's side of the family was old Melbourne money, and her second cousin, as heir to a vast newspaper and magazine empire, was rolling in it. When Molly married McBride and became a mere schoolteacher, her side of the clan slipped from the horizon, although they were always invited to extended family functions, as often as not attended by famous actors, prominent businessmen and politicians on the make, and, on one occasion, the prime minister of the day. Not that Lucy ever met them, but she had rubbed shoulders with such people and, in this way, was at least familiar with what the tabloids called 'society'. The abundance of society's money, however, was less familiar, so while staying at five-star hotels was written into Molly's psyche, the price of doing so was not necessarily written into her bank account. Because of such extravagances, the fanciful romantic in Lucy, which was practically all of her, fancied her side of the extended family as a kind of faded, colonial aristocracy, affecting habits and attitudes that no longer bore any relation to the facts of their lives.

And so they stayed at the Gritti Palace, dined at Florian's and drank at Harry's Bar. But it was a mixed experience. Lucy was all too conscious of tagging along after her parents, feeling that they still thought of her as a child, and being consumed with a desire to break away from the fold. Tempers flared more than once, earning Lucy her childhood nickname of 'madam' all over again. 'Madam' for the imperious manner that she affected when her parents or the world had let her down; 'madam' for the tantrums she had once been famous for and which had returned a couple of times during the trip. Then, one night, when she could feel the temper of 'madam' rising in her, she told her parents that she would wander off by herself, and McBride and Molly, aware of the tension in her eyes, let her be. But she didn't tell them, either then or later, where she was going, for it was on this night that she saw Fortuny's house for the first time and, purely by accident, Fortuny himself. She was sixteen.

She had stood, that evening, in a small square between an art gallery and a waterway that ran into the Grand Canal. The traghetto crossed the canal at this point, and there was a wooden stop to her left where customers waited to be ferried over to the Calle Del Traghetto on the other side. The air was fresh and she had stood leaning against an iron lamppost in the square's centre, staring up at the balcony of Fortuny's house. People passed her, some turning to stare at the young woman gazing up at the lighted houses, the palazzos large and small, that lined the opposite side of the canal. She didn't mind and showed no sign of caring. They moved on, and she continued watching.

Then, with the moored boats bobbing on the canal before her, amid the tinkle and low talk of distant outdoor diners, a figure stepped out onto the balcony of the *piano nobile*, stood for a moment under the white pointed arches, then sat, observing the lights on the water. He was neither short nor tall, broad across the chest from years of playing, but lean also, his parted silvery hair falling to the sides, just as she'd imagined. A woman appeared, only briefly, but Lucy could see her stooped stance and make out her hair, which was drawn back tightly about her scalp.

The woman placed something on a small table and was then gone. The man lifted a small cup, sipped from it, and when he replaced it on the table Lucy could have sworn she heard the sound of the cup touching the saucer. He was dwarfed by the row of Arabian arches, a shadowy figure, indistinct. But it was Fortuny all right. She moved forward, just a little, keeping clear of the lamplight along the walkway, then stood still, staring across the canal, her eyes straining in the night. She stayed there until the figure on the balcony rose and re-entered the house. As the windows were closed she turned, the square suddenly dark and deserted. Lucy then strolled slowly back to the hotel, her heart thumping in her chest like some piece of industrial machinery gone mad and about to explode.

She never told her parents about this secret world of hers, and in later years wished she'd found a way to do so. But how could she? It was in the nature of this world, this most enchanting of myths, not to be shared or spoken of. But the pressure that built up inside her from carrying its weight, from simply being at what certain novels she read called the 'awkward' age, often burst from her without warning. And no time was worse than when they returned from that trip.

Molly, who'd put a series of headaches down to the tension of travelling and an early summer heatwave, suddenly collapsed and died one steamy January morning. Nobody was in the house, Dr McBride was at work, Lucy at school, and Molly died alone. It was two months after their return from Europe, and the weeks leading up to her mother's death had been marred with 'scenes', none more wretched to Lucy than those nights when she barely knew what was happening to her or what she was doing. She had taken to smoking cigarettes and wearing revealing clothes that even Molly, who prided herself on being an enlightened mother, was shocked by. But Lucy, driven by forces that she barely comprehended, walked the streets tossed between the desire to be gazed upon and the revulsion of being leered at.

Molly went on about it, again and again, about this daughter of hers, about her ways, about her walk. The lingering memory of the summer was the sound of the screen door slapping in the night and Lucy, on reflection, forever storming from the house.

Then Molly was suddenly dead. Incomprehensibly gone, no more, and Lucy was filled with the shame that she didn't feel at the time but would feel for years after. Week after week, month after month, she craved Molly, if only to take back that summer, to make everything right again, and this time be the dutiful daughter that her mother had lacked just when the dutiful daughter was needed most. I'll be good, she promised the empty rooms of the house. I'll be good.

And it was then that playing became far more than just a straightforward pleasure. For it was in the playing that Lucy forgot. And at certain moments during those long early months after her mother's death, when she closed her eyes and the music became inaudible even to her, like a pain grown too intense to be registered by the body or the mind, she came to feel what she could only describe as nothingness. A blissful annihilation. For it was guilt that plagued Lucy—a guilt that both father and daughter suffered. Dr McBride never forgave himself for not spotting his wife's symptoms, for failing to save his own. Nobody ever told you about the guilt. Not even books. They told you about the crying and the wailing and the sadness when someone died, but not the guilt. Lucy could remember only the bad things for ages after, the times the difficult daughter had vented her exasperation on her mother. And the childhood assumption that everything and everyone would still be there in the morning, and the next, and the next after that, stretching out to infinity, was shattered.

It was only in playing that all of that, the pain, the guilt, everything, was obliterated. And it was only when she emerged from long, intense sessions in her room, in the strangely quiet house, that she would feel her fingers on the strings and register the aching of her muscles; only then that she would be tired and ready for sleep.

Gradually, night after night, it became easier to feel nothing until… Till, in the end, it became the simplest thing in the world: she just closed her eyes and played until the playing took over. And it was always the music of Fortuny she went to. The anger, the sudden jabs of the bow, the raw energy and the long, hanging notes, played out but somehow lingering into the next phrase. It was always Fortuny's music that kept her there in that silence. She knew it was a kind of death, and every evening she welcomed a little dying because without it, she felt sure, she would have died altogether. And slowly, without realising or noting the shadow line, the nights, the days, the mornings and afternoons all became easier to accept. Even the sun slanting through the green trees became thrilling once more, and hope, that part of her life she'd thrown away, came back to her. Insistent and imploring.

But those nights, with her father—quickly grown thin and with a permanent lost look in his eyes now—listening from a far room as she played, would always remain with her. And a part of her, in the years to follow, would always remain the girl who never forgave herself, the girl who promised to be good if only, and if only… The girl who played the cello, night after night, in order to feel absolutely nothing. There would even be a time, years later when the ache in heart had dulled, when she would secretly long for it all again, long for the pain to return. A pain like that worth dying a little for every night.

So when Lucy finally took that long walk to the stage of the Conservatorium in Venice, difficult as it was, she had not only groomed herself for just such a walk over the last ten years, life had prepared her, steeled her, for it. She breathed in deeply, glimpsing the upright figure of Fortuny as she did, right-hand side, third from the front, on the aisle, then exhaled.

She remembered only the opening notes and the applause at the end but nothing in between. Nothing was easy to feel. Life had prepared her well. She placed the cello back on its stand and retraced her steps over the creaking stage to the same canvas seat, quickly brushing her hair back from her face as she sat, allowing herself the briefest of glances at Fortuny, who was gazing into the distance, seemingly oblivious to everything around him.

When the recital finished soon after, the hall quickly filled with chatter. It seemed everyone was talking over each other. Lucy paid no attention. She looked, nervously, for Fortuny, only to see his black coat disappearing through the main door at the back of the hall. The noise of the hall was suddenly unbearable as, in a panic, she watched his retreating figure. And somewhere in the crowd, the words of a young man named Marco were just audible.

Chapter Five

IT WAS Marco who had met her at the station when she'd arrived a few weeks before. And it was Marco who, in the days and weeks that followed, introduced her to *his* Venice, as apart from the one she had, until then, briefly visited, or merely observed in books or become familiar with through maps. She had arrived by train late in the afternoon. The Grand Canal was cluttered with vaporetti—'little steamers'; she smiled, quietly translating the word into English—the water buses of the city, lumbering whales among the swift and agile taxis, as well as the city's many boats of trade and pleasure.

She'd been sitting there for almost an hour, her cello beside her and a large canvas suitcase her father had bought her as a farewell present at her feet. (Their farewell had been simple: a brave smile on her father's lips, but not in his eyes, as he said goodbye to the last of the family, the last of the old life.) She dwelt on that smile now, on the memory of the family, the three of them. They had been a world unto themselves, and, looking back, she could see it was always a danger, that neither Molly nor McBride would have any other world to embrace when theirs collapsed.

The steps were cold, the air chilly, but she sat still and waited, home thoughts giving way to the excitement of arrival as she scanned the waterway where fallen rendering from the buildings revealed the brickwork beneath. Moss and seaweed had collected about the base of the red and white 'barbershop' mooring poles and on the steps of the doorways; statues were caked with a green film; wood rotted at the waterside; washing hung on pulley lines, and an old woman's chin rested on a window sill. And in the air, the smell of seaweed and sewage forever the lingering scent of this unique city, this sinking, crumbling wonder that was Venice.

And so Lucy sat, her hand resting on the black cello case, waiting for it all to begin. The real thing. Waiting to step into the world that she was convinced life had prepared her for, a life she was certain she had been born to join.

But while she stared at the grey façade of San Simeon Piccolo, at the Hotel Carlton, the ticket stalls, the packed vaporetti, the workers in their uniform blue overalls, the men in business suits carrying rich, leather briefcases, it suddenly occurred to her that this throng of people was coming away from a day's work. Lucy rested her chin in her hand and reflected that this was a working city, whose workers now hurried past its churches and bridges as anywhere else they would pass by sandwich shops or bus stops without a second glance. She leaned back on the steps, watched the faded oranges, pinks and yellows of the buildings mingling with the late sun, listened to the constant slapping of waves on the canal and the rattle of the luggage trolleys merging with the loudspeaker of the railway station. The long hours of the journey at last beginning to affect her, Lucy almost gave up waiting, and began eyeing the hotels nearest the station.

She wondered if she'd been overlooked on the crowded steps but, no, her cello was her emblem. She was the new girl. She took a chocolate from her carry bag and as she unwrapped it a voice beside her said, 'Excuse me?'

A young man, his English slow and deliberate, was standing next to her.

'Signorina—Miss McBride?'

'Lucy.' She stood up, smiling, extending her hand, and the young man returned the smile, possibly amused at the sight of a young woman offering to shake hands with him.

'Welcome,' he said, 'I am Marco, Marco Mazetti. But I am late. I am sorry.'

'Don't be.' She looked about, gestured. 'It's been lovely to wait.'

Marco smiled again and waved his hand expansively across the view, as if it were a painting and he were the artist.

'You like it?'

A fat evening sun, a rich orange yolk just behind her, was hanging over Cannaregio, and Lucy turned precisely at the moment that it touched the rooftops and bled itself onto the tiles, trickling the last of its light into the lanes, the calles and canals of the city. Lucy smiled.

'Yes. I like it.'

She picked up her cello, Marco lifted her suitcase. Together they walked down the steps to the canal, where they took a rolling, crowded waterbus that stirred the murky waters washed in from the Dead Lagoon, then continued on the long curve that took it down to San Marco, till eventually, circling the city, it would arrive back where it had started.

They alighted at the San Stae stop and crossed a small square in front of the vast, chalky columns of San Stae itself. From there, they followed a narrow passage lane and passed a doorway in which an old woman, her shopping bags by her side, had squatted to urinate. Marco looked away, possibly embarrassed, but Lucy stared openly as the old woman, too, looked down at her own feet, seemingly fascinated by the progress of the yellow stream that flowed from her body. Further along, the passage opened onto a small square where children were playing soccer against a wall while their parents sat on chairs and benches, smoking, watching, and sipping small drinks.

'This is your square.' Marco smiled. 'It is a nice square.'

Lucy nodded and they crossed the nice square to a quiet, narrow canal. They followed it a short way, then Marco came to a stop.

'Here.' he nodded. 'This is it.' He put her suitcase down and once more smiled when Lucy extended her hand again as she thanked him.

He handed her an envelope that contained the key, then wrote something on the back of a card.

'This is my telephone number and address. If you have any difficulties…' He paused a moment, constructing the sentence. 'Be sure to call.' Clearly pleased with his English idiom, he bowed slightly and set off in the direction of the square.

Alone now, with shadows falling across the steep walls, the windows and the small balconies of the houses, Lucy lingered at the door of her new home, closing her eyes and allowing herself a moment of absolute stillness before finally turning the key.

That night she slept without even bothering to unpack or eat. At one stage she woke, phantom shapes and unfamiliar shadows around her, and lay quiet and still in the puzzling, nameless darkness of the city, until her conscious mind told her where she was and she closed her eyes again, drifting back into the leaden sleep of the traveller.

But the bells woke her. Every church, every square, every chapel and bell tower in the city rang in the day. Near and far, clear and faint, they boomed, clanged, rumbled and chimed through chord and discord, melodic order and musical chaos, a jumble of rhythms stumbling in and out of each other until the last bells finally collapsed into silence, tapering off into the distance like the jangle of loose change.

The city was still waking when she walked down to the square. The cafés were just opening, bread, cakes, croissants and fruit were being delivered in hand-held carts. And in the cool, bright stillness of the air, which carried the scent of coffee, the clatter and chatter of daily commerce, and the occasional slap of the canal waters, Lucy smiled to herself and yawned in half-sleepy delight.

She followed the main streets, over the wide, sweeping span of the as yet deserted Rialto then, still dreamy, roamed into one of the lanes that led off it. Aimless, feeling lost, and wishing she'd remembered her map, she drifted past the shopfronts, the metal awnings, the clothes, the leather ware, the masks, the tourist gifts of the city, until she finally stumbled out into the Piazza San Marco. She had been here before, but all the same she stood silent—her eyes, wide with wonder, roving over the vast open spaces of the square, vacant apart from a few city cleaners and two or three early-morning commuters. Quietly, she told herself over and over again, that in all the work, the humdrum and the sheer tedium that would inevitably be part of the days, months and years to come, she must never forget this moment.

By mid-morning, she stood under a cool, blue sky at the southern end of the Campo San Stefano, shaking her head. That couldn't be it. Not *that*. Marco was laughing. Yes, yes, he insisted. That was it, this rundown Renaissance palace really was the Conservatorium. Its marble, its stone, was no longer white, but stained grey and black by smoke and weather, as if brushed with charcoal. Weeds were growing from the first-floor balcony, where fat pigeons nestled, flapping into position on top of the portal columns or on the crown of the gargoyle head above the front door. With its grey stone and its iron grille windows, the building looked more like a disused prison than a music school.

There were no signs, no plaques outside, no indication of what the building's function might be, only a large wooden board dangling from a window stating that the Department of Labour was carrying out renovations. Marco started to speak, but his words were lost in a sudden thunder of rubble that cascaded down from the third floor through a long, plastic chute into the open courtyard. It was as if the building were col-

lapsing in on itself as they watched, and Lucy had arrived in time to witness its death rattle. They waited
for the noise to settle, then Marco led her upstairs to
the salon of the *primo piano*. This was more like it, she
thought, and breathed a sigh of satisfaction and
thanksgiving as she looked about her, realising that the
room was almost intimidating in its grandeur. She almost skated over the glassy surface of the marble floor,
under golden chandeliers, sporting angels and the
tumbling heavenly clouds and deep blue sky of the
painted ceiling that looked, at first sight, like a vast,
suspended wedding cake.

Marco introduced her to a woman seated at a small
desk in the salon, who took her name and disappeared
into an adjoining room. As she waited, Lucy paced
about the room, staring at the paintings on the walls,
the frescos on the ceilings, all the while conscious of
the clipped echo of her shoes on the marble floor.

When the secretary returned she told Lucy that Signor Bellini, her teacher whom she had come to meet,
was not in that day and that she should return in the
morning. It was then that Marco showed her around.
She heard, from a further room, the high, thrilling
voice of a soprano rippling across her scales, and then
the sound of a piano. Lucy closed her eyes for moment
and when she opened them was, once again, staring at
one of the many faded rococo ceilings of the elegantly
faded Palazzo Pisani, her new school. Somewhere, a

violinist played Bach, the soprano tripped across her exercises, the piano swelled, tinkled, rumbled, and Lucy looked about, quietly thrilling to the pastiche, the jumble, the sanctuary of sound. And hovering somewhere, amongst the sounds, the rooms, the painted ceilings, the long marble fireplaces, the gilded, scratchy mirrors etched with the initials of former students and lovers, and the wide, lead-light windows that looked out onto a quiet, domestic canal, was the real, the physical, possibility of Fortuny.

For this was Fortuny's school. He had taught here, given talks here, performed recitals here. He had, unquestionably and on numerous occasions, walked over this same shiny marble floor, and would certainly have taught in, or passed through, the room where she now stood. Every doorway, every window, every faded mirror suggested his proximity.

Back in the Campo San Stefano, they sat on the steps at the base of the square's central statue. Marco stared up and then asked, 'Do you know this statue?' She shook her head. He laughed quickly, privately enjoying a joke before sharing it. 'This is Nicolò Tommaseo. Say hello.' He grinned, as Lucy nodded to the statue. 'This man was a heroic figure against the Austrians. He was also a scholar. And this is his monument.'

Lucy looked respectfully at the substantial statue of the nineteenth-century bearded figure, an impressive pile of sculpted books behind his legs.

'But look.' Marco took her arm and led her to the side of the statue. 'From here he appears to be…' He paused, getting the phrase right. 'Shitting books. Yes?'

'Yes.' She nodded, suddenly laughing. 'Yes, he does.'

They looked at Nicolò Tommaseo for a few moments longer, then Marco led her towards a large café on the other side of the square, saying, 'It's known locally as *caga libri*. The Bookshitter. It's good,' he said, laughing again as they approached the café. 'I like it. Sounds better in English. I just love English.'

In her flat that night, Lucy dragged raw, rasping notes from her cello, hitting the strings with the bow as if slapping someone's face or smacking the notes into life before entering the melody. All new students at the school had to perform a small piece for the staff and fellow students. It was something of a tradition, an introduction. And Lucy had chosen *Allemande*, No. 2, from the Bach Suites, the piece that had roused her from her slumbers in that faraway garden ten years before. There were many ways of approaching the suite, but she had always played it Fortuny's way, and always with confidence, but now she approached it with apprehension for she knew that *he* would be in the audience when she played in a week's time. There, physically, in the concert hall, and she would, at last, play to Fortuny. She continued to practise, anxious and a little frightened, but knowing that she was ready, that life had prepared her well, and that that day couldn't come soon enough.

Now that concert was over. Students, teachers and friends talked excitedly of their own and everybody else's performances. No one seemed to have left the hall, no one, that is, except Fortuny. And to Lucy, still in a panic, his absence made the hall empty. Marco was complimenting her on her playing, her manner, but she left him in mid-sentence, left her cello where it stood, left the group of students that had gathered round her, and rushed towards the door.

Down the steep marble stairs she went, following Fortuny to the ground floor, brushing past students and teachers, only just managing to stay with the Maestro's short but surprisingly swift strides. He disappeared into the grey courtyard and crossed into the *portego* of the Conservatorium, but when Lucy reached the door of the *portego* she was held back by two workers carrying long planks of wooden scaffolding. Outside, the lean frame of Fortuny swept over the stones of the square facing the school. Lucy pushed forward.

And as she ran across the smooth stones of the Campiello Pisano, an inner voice was urging her: *Go on, call out. Say the word, say 'maestro', and everything else will follow. Go on.* But she remained mute and it seemed that the moment would pass and be done with forever and Lucy would remain the girl who had waited a lifetime of summers but, in the end, said nothing. She couldn't do it, wasn't born for such a moment of daring. Not Lucy, perhaps somebody else. And as she watched the receding figure of Fortuny, she felt the moment, and all those years, slipping away from her.

And so, after all, she called. Spoke the word from which everything else would follow. 'Maestro,' she called, and the dark figure in front halted and turned towards her.

Lucy slowed and now stood before him. Her hair was blown back, her face flushed from the sudden exertion; his face bore a trace of annoyance, that of a man (but she couldn't have known this) who hadn't slept well the night before. Fortuny stared at her enquiringly, still frowning, as she greeted him and introduced herself in a distracting accent he couldn't quite place. But he knew her all right. She was the girl who had just played his music, she was the wave who had just lifted his heart, and given him this dull sweet ache which he had carried with him out into the square.

Then she fell silent. Fortuny said nothing, not wishing to encourage conversation because, as much as this young woman had moved him, he also feared her. And as much as he told himself that he had no reason to fear a young woman he had never met before, the dull, sweet ache under his heart told him otherwise.

He nodded, his expression indicating that she should get on with it.

'Signor Fortuny,' she began, 'I won't keep you long. You must have many students approaching you for advice, but I have admired your work for a very long time.'

Again Fortuny nodded without speaking, the tolerant air of the master who had heard it all before. There was another awkward silence and Lucy looked down at the stones of the square, almost afraid to look up again.

'Please forgive me, Maestro, but I'd very much like to know what you thought of my playing.'

Fortuny frowned, seemed displeased, as if he was unused to such forwardness.

'I don't mean to annoy you,' she suddenly added, realising that nothing was going to plan.

Fortuny cleared his throat. 'I thought,' he said, considering his words very carefully, his voice surprisingly quiet, but guttural, 'you were very entertaining.'

'Is that all?' she blurted out, and immediately wished to die. But he spoke before she could make amends.

'You have a long way to go.'

'I know.' She lowered her eyes, then looked up to see Fortuny smile as he repeated himself.

'A long way.'

The smile was still on his face, and he wasn't moving. She ventured another question.

'How far?'

The smile faded and he shrugged.

'How far do you want to go?'

'I want to be the best. Like you.'

'Yes, the best,' he said, and laughed briefly.

It was, Lucy noted, a wise laugh. A laugh that had heard it all before. His tiredness was not apparent to her. His eyes sparkled, his smile—amused, sympathetic, all-knowing—that of a man who knew life in a way that most were not privileged to experience it: the way of those who have been somewhere extraordinary and come back with stardust upon them; who were not simply carried along by the events of life, but who created them. Those who lived on their own terms, mixing it with the gods and causing Destiny to change its plans.

'I'm prepared to work hard,' she said, almost pleading.

Fortuny looked about the square as if, Lucy thought, he was searching for an end to the conversation. But he then turned to her, his eyes narrowing.

'Do you have a strong will?'

She said nothing.

'Strong,' he repeated, his voice rising, his arms gesturing to emphasise the point.

'Yes,' she said, trying to sound confident but clearly uncertain of his meaning.

'Then I wish you all the best.'

He turned to leave but Lucy, feeling cheated, stopped him again. He turned to face her once more, and she noticed that they were the same height, that their faces were level. She also noted the sweep of his hair, and the moody eyes into which she had stared throughout the eternity of her adolescence.

'Maestro, I know you sometimes give classes.'

'Not any more.'

But Lucy was not to be denied.

'Please. Please let me play for you,' she persisted. 'And if, at the end, you can see no point, then so be it.'

He paused, looking this determined young woman up and down, then eyed the comings and goings of the large, familiar square to his left as he considered the matter, his fingers lightly tapping his thighs.

'Your name is?'

'Lucy McBride.'

Another pause, and then he gave her a small card and named a time, something in the manner of a doctor arranging an appointment, as her father would, then turned and continued across the square towards the shops on the other side.

Lucy watched him go, then closed her eyes and held the card to her before walking back under the pointed, gargoyle arch of the school's door. Inside, she rejoined Marco and the other students whom she had so quickly left only a few minutes before, and made her apologies. As they descended the stairs, Marco once again imparted his observations about her playing, but even though she smiled, she hadn't the faintest idea of what he'd just said.

That night Fortuny walked restlessly from one end of his salon to the other. Had it been summer, or even a mild spring, he could have stepped into the courtyard, sat beneath the lilacs and whiled away the evening. But it was raining and the heating had only just taken the chill out of the air. Rosa was visiting her parents. There was no food prepared and she would not return till morning.

His footsteps were the only sound in the salon. He stopped at his cello, ran his fingers over the shiny polished wood and thought, for the first time since morning, about the young woman at the Conservatorium. He had no desire to receive students again, but she had moved him and he still felt that wave or, rather, that swell, which might somewhere become a wave. Were they that different, these young women, or was it just that he was no longer young? he wondered. And did their eyes imply that they might dismantle you even as they desired you, or did the eyes of the young always say that? But she had played, not so much well as with unmistakeable energy, and, if he cared to admit it, he'd found her refreshing. Yes, she had life. She had life all right. Sometimes, rather too much of it. But those rough edges could be smoothed out. Besides, she would be a young voice in the salon and the house was in need of young voices. He sat smoking, a practice his doctor had forbidden him, and thought of the morning's events while casting an occasional eye over the Venus on the wall.

A little later, Fortuny sat at a round walnut table in his study, idly tracing the line of his family tree. The chart, carefully drawn on parchment, was spread out. His fingers moved slowly over the centuries, pausing at points on the chart where branches of the family stopped, then moving on to where others started. His fingers came to rest on the final entry, his own. He circled his name, whispered it into the air, 'Fortuny, the Great Full Stop' (a manner of address he fell into in moods such as these), then he drew an invisible line from his name to the vacant space beneath.

When he finally retired that night it was late. He had eaten nothing, but had drunk a small glass of spirits—Calvados, his favourite. For the last time that evening the silent house echoed to his footsteps, and as he switched the lamps off, he became aware of the need to fill it with other sounds.

Chapter Six

THE thing had been done, and Lucy sat marvelling at the events of the day like a spectator, as if she were the distant, reported figure in a particularly interesting anecdote. She felt as though she had successfully communicated with Mars, and took Fortuny's card from her wallet, holding it tight just to reassure herself that the encounter of the morning had really taken place.

And Fortuny himself? Well, she knew now that they were the same height and that their eyes were disconcertingly level when they spoke. She remembered his lean frame, and his broad chest that spoke of a lifetime's playing. Indeed, it was his physical bearing that had surprised her—that didn't come across in photographs and which few interviewers mentioned. But there, in his very presence, was a sense of strength and power. Yes, power. Not merely conferred by his position but in the aura around the man himself. As well as this, she remembered the dignity of his posture and carriage, his swift and agile movements and gestures, like those of a man twenty years younger. All of this she recalled, as well as that lingering sense of someone who had been somewhere extraordinary, who didn't need to say where, because it was in their eyes.

When Fortuny woke he was still tired. He rarely slept well lately, but when he did close his eyes sleep was not the balm it had once been. In the mornings he always examined his face in the mirror before going downstairs where Rosa would have prepared a simple breakfast.

When Carla, an old friend, visited that morning she remarked on how young he looked. So many of their friends and former associates, she said, had succumbed to age, but not Fortuny. He lost his tiredness momentarily, until she left, lingering at the door, looking about the room as if committing it to memory. Carla's blonde hair had been tied back, her skin had a solarium tan, and her fingers, as always, were covered with the gold and diamond rings which Fortuny knew to be the last of her wealth, her husband having died a bankrupt. She waved goodbye from the courtyard below and, when she was gone, Fortuny retired to an armchair to admire his specially made, seven-panelled windows.

The week before he had committed himself to a meeting with this new student at the Conservatorium. Now he waited for the girl to arrive, vaguely aware of a mixture of longing and apprehension that her impending visit had aroused, and dwelling on the unsettling nostalgia that her playing had awakened in him. The thought now irritated him and he suddenly wished he'd never agreed to the whole business.

Lately, Fortuny had been a man nagged by doubts, troubled by the space between the dreams he held for life and the waking reality that his productive years had created. He was, after all, a retired artist, and all that was left now was the summing up. It was that time, the arrival of which he had always dreaded, when what he set out do would be measured against what he had already done. His life, like the trophies on display in his study, would stand or fall according to how he felt about himself whenever he entered the room. Which was why Fortuny rarely went to his study, with its framed photographs, its boxes of correspondence, cuttings and mementos; why he rarely indulged in the dangerous drug of nostalgia.

The girl, Lucy McBride, arrived, punctually. Rosa brought in a small plate of cakes and creams and placed them on a table with a pot of coffee. She filled their cups and left the room, where Fortuny sipped his coffee in the silence that followed and Lucy looked slowly about the room she already knew so well from photographs.

She was amazed at the familiarity of it all, the order of it. Everything was where it should be, where her imagination, her memory, would have had it. She had stepped into the chamber of her own dreams, crossed the landscape of an intensely private mythological region for the first time, and came to it all as if her presence completed the scene. It was as though everything—the room itself, everything within it, even the coffee cups—had waited for exactly this moment to arrive in order to achieve completion. And with the curtains drawn closed, partitioning the salon to create the effect of a private chamber, the atmosphere was even intimate. The room contained what in the photographs had always appeared to Lucy to be a bishop's robe. And it was. There were dark, wooden cabinets and engraved chairs; paintings hung end to end on the white walls; a long couch was heaped with coloured cushions; there was a piano and, of course, a cello. Fortuny sat in a small armchair, Lucy on the piano stool.

He seemed to possess a physical presence beyond his dimensions, and as he spoke she noted the strength of his forearms and his large hands, their knuckles prominent. Almost, she thought, workman's hands, as if the earthiness of his playing was a natural extension of them.

Fortuny observed her for a moment. Her blue eyes, her blue jeans, her hair tied in what he remembered the Americans calling a ponytail, her lack of cosmetics, the natural tan of her skin. It was a look Fortuny was not accustomed to seeing in a city whose sophistication was often overblown and cloying. Her handbag had been dumped by the side of the piano stool.

At last he spoke. 'Where is your music?'

His voice was abrupt, his manner impatient, his accent difficult. Lucy had just bitten into a cake.

'In my head.'

'Your head?'

She swallowed. 'I don't use sheets,' she said, knowing she was speaking too quickly but unable to slow down. 'Only at the beginning. When I can play something five times without a mistake, I've memorised it. That's my test.'

She came to a sudden stop and Fortuny smiled. It had also been his test. The girl was nervous, which surprised him because she had shown no sign of nerves the previous week at the recital. Besides, he had convinced himself that these young women didn't have nerves. Oddly, her anxiety relaxed him. Not that it was obvious but, having conducted, played and taught all over Europe he recognised the signs. He relaxed her with conversation, asked her brief questions about her background, her country (Australia, which solved the puzzle of the accent he couldn't quite place), her school of study, how long she had been in Venice. And gradually her speech slowed, became more natural until, eventually, she even asked questions of Fortuny himself.

'Do you still play?'

'Not publicly.'

'But for yourself?'

'Only sometimes. For practice,' he said, noting the untouched cup beside her. 'You don't drink coffee?'

'Yes,' she said, having forgotten all about it.

'Then drink.'

She quickly sipped it, then placed the cup back on the saucer.

'Good?'

'Very good,' she said, smiling for the first time.

'Rosa's coffee is famous.'

'So is Signor Fortuny. I've admired your work…' Lucy paused. 'For many years now.'

Fortuny nodded, settling back in his chair as Lucy continued, asking him about the musicians *he* had admired as a young man.

And in the ten minutes that followed, Fortuny began to realise something else about this young woman: she had spoken of nothing but music. Music and musicians. Their techniques, their little tricks, their hours and patterns of practice. She passed no comments about his house, as most students would have done. Indeed, she seemed almost indifferent to it. They sat in a room without windows and her world seemed to exclude anything but music, just as the room itself excluded the distractions of the outside world. She had all the single-minded concentration, the hunger, the eyes of a truly ambitious artist.

There it was again, nostalgia, the word ringing like a random bell in the night. For a moment he was distracted, suddenly filled with an uncharacteristic yearning for those hungry years, the hours of training, secretly developing a craft, the long nights, the solitude, the successes, the past rivalries and the friendships. And the energy, now spent; the achievements, now taken for granted; the massive act of will that had meant pushing aside all other considerations, all extraneous living. This pleasant, engaging young woman possessed it all.

But it was only when Lucy was playing that he understood the sense of familiarity he had experienced a week earlier at the Conservatorium, understood it properly and recognised at last his own style in hers. This young woman was not only familiar with his work but had clearly taken his technique as her own. It was both gratifying and oddly disturbing, but he sat perfectly still throughout her playing.

When she had finished, she performed a simple act, a gesture, that literally took Fortuny's breath away. She knelt before him on the floor. It was something Lucy had been used to doing from an early age. She always knelt or sat in that manner, always preferred the space, the expanse of the floor, to the constrictions of a chair. She finished playing, paused for a moment to let the last, lingering notes fade, put the cello on its rest, then simply slid off the practice stool and onto the Persian rug beneath her, tossing her hair back as she did so. In her pressed, faded blue jeans, Lucy momentarily forgot where she was and thought nothing of kneeling on Fortuny's floor.

To Fortuny, in its ease, its natural grace, its unself-conscious youthfulness, it seemed one of the most entrancing sights he'd seen in a long time. Nobody, he suddenly felt, not one of his guests over all the years, had ever done such a thing in quite the same way. Again, as had happened at the recital the previous week, a deep, green wave passed briefly through the room. Silent. Over the marble floor, over the chair in which Fortuny sat, over Fortuny. No, not a wave, but a swell. A swell of the deepest green that would somewhere become a wave.

Lucy watched as Fortuny seemed to slump forward in his chair, coughing violently. He dropped his cup on the floor and his hands gripped his sides. She jumped up, held him by a shoulder with one hand, and patted his back with the other until, slowly, his breathing returned to normal. He sat back in the chair while Lucy cautiously resumed her position on the rug, concern evident in her eyes.

Fortuny had been made suddenly human, and, of course, she remained completely unaware of what she had done. His poise had been suddenly shattered, the cup had dropped, and she had held him—the Maestro, Fortuny—held him to her. To Fortuny, it was confirmation that these young women might very well undo you, even as they desired you, for it almost seemed that she had struck the first blow and part of him was already, quietly, asking himself if she would strike the last.

But he made light of the episode while he wiped his mouth with his handkerchief, embroidered with a blue crescent: the family monogram that Lucy recognised, knew from many years before when Fortuny had responded to her letter with a brief note. That same crescent which, she saw now, decorated the wall hangings in the salon, visible on his handkerchief as he lightly touched his forehead.

On no account was she even to think about picking up the broken pieces of the cup and saucer lying on the marble floor, he told her. He stuffed the handkerchief back into his breast pocket and called Rosa. When she came, Fortuny indicated the floor, muttered small apologies, then waited in silence till she was gone.

'Now,' he said at last, swallowing and quickly composing himself in his armchair. 'You would like lessons?'

'Yes,' Lucy said quickly. 'I'm quite prepared to pay.' And then winced inwardly. Perhaps she shouldn't have mentioned the vulgar matter of money. But, then, she quickly consoled herself, Fortuny was a true Venetian after all, and money was never a vulgar topic in Venice.

Fortuny, however, ignored the remark, and asked, 'Who is your instructor at the school?'

'Signor Bellini.'

'Ah, Bellini…' Fortuny sighed, looking up towards the sky-blue ceiling. 'He's good.'

'Yes.'

'Quite good,' Fortuny added, having privately pronounced the man a hack all his life, and with a faint smile in his eyes that seemed to say, *Good, but not good enough, eh?*

It was quite a jolt to see the young woman staring straight back at him, her eyes directly meeting his. This young woman was clearly no fool and had read the faint smile on his lips with unerring accuracy. To Lucy, it was as simple as deciphering her father's code of compliments. In her father's lexicon, 'throwing yourself into it' meant 'good'. He had often observed of her playing that she 'threw herself into it' and that he liked that. But in Fortuny's system of judgement, 'good' clearly meant 'bad'. Or worse.

In this way, their first tacit agreement was reached, with the most barely perceptible of nods. Their duplicitous collusion acknowledged, Fortuny continued.

'You've told Bellini about coming here?'

'Yes,' Lucy lied.

'Good.' Fortuny nodded, recognising the lie as he looked away, appearing to study the curtains. 'It is a matter a courtesy.'

He turned back to face her, and in a brusque, businesslike manner quickly listed a number of faults in her playing.

'You rush.'

'I know.'

'You hurry phrases.'

'I know.'

'Stop saying "I know". You don't,' Fortuny suddenly snapped, his voice no longer soft but harsh and guttural. 'If you knew you would have corrected it.'

Lucy said nothing.

'You over-emphasise the light and the dark.'

She nodded, on the verge of saying 'I know', but checked herself.

'Have you ever seen an actor go from quiet sobbing to shrieking with nothing in between and nowhere left to go?'

'Yes.'

'Well, you should have learnt from it.' Fortuny's voice rose and fell. 'You have to control the light and the dark. You understand?'

She nodded again, still kneeling on the rug but looking about the room as if preparing to leave. In fact, she was suddenly overcome by a delayed sense of the immensity of being in Fortuny's house, being with him, talking to him.

'Do you still want lessons?'

Fortuny broke the spell and she looked up, clearly puzzled by the question.

'Yes.'

Fortuny eyed her, calculating his words.

'I will say hard things, difficult things.'

'I know.'

'But they will need to be said. I teach adults, not children.'

'I'm not a child.' Lucy's face rose like that of a defiant child.

The merest hint of a smile glinted in Fortuny's eyes. 'I will remind you of that,' he said. 'If you can't take the things I will need to say then you must leave now.'

Fortuny then spoke for ten minutes about Lucy's technique and in that time said nothing complimentary. He was, she finally concluded, letting her know who was boss.

'You've got life. There's no doubt about that,' and repeated the word 'life' with a quiet reflectiveness, as if it were uncommon enough but hardly rare. He looked up at her sharply. 'But subtlety,' he said, shaking his head. 'We're going to have to teach you that.'

When Lucy walked out of the salon door and onto the steps that led down into the courtyard, Fortuny's words stayed with her. She had no doubt that he had deliberately tried to bully her to test her resolve, her stamina, to see what she could take and what she couldn't. Bullied her to establish whether she had not only the will required but also the capacity to hear strong and harsh criticism; to have her work analysed, torn apart, then painstakingly put back together again. Could she do that? If not, he would, presumably, be wasting his time. Well, he'd soon find out. It had been her first test, the first tug in a tug of war, and as she strode across the courtyard to the large, wooden gate, she was determined to meet any other tests he might throw at her.

While Lucy was closing the gate, Fortuny was standing in front of one of the baroque salon mirrors, its golden frame caught by the light, his face indistinct in the faded glass. He was smoothing his hair, and when he had finished took the handkerchief from his breast pocket, folded it, refolded it, then placed it back in the pocket in such a way as to suggest to himself and anybody else that it had never been used and the coughing fit had never taken place.

That done, he stepped back, took one final look at his reflection and straightened his shoulders, then turned and walked towards the white, marble steps that led to the hallway, onto the *portego*, and out into the residential part of the house.

Back at her flat after her visit to Fortuny, Lucy played and replayed a selection of works throughout the whole afternoon. She played until her back, legs and arms ached, until her fingers became slow and sluggish and she could no longer manoeuvre the bow. Then she began again, but every time she played it seemed worse than ever. Fortuny was right. She was just another hack, with a bit more life in her than the others but a hack all the same. Oh, he'd never said it, but he'd meant it all right. When she was finally exhausted she rose from the cello, put on her coat and stomped out into the quiet evening light. She walked through the tiny winding passages and streets of Santa Croce then down into the Campo San Polo, where families were enjoying the late afternoon sun while their children kicked soccer balls against the medieval walls of the houses.

It was cool but the spring air was clear. She walked through dark, narrow lanes, where the buildings often seemed to incline towards each other like forlorn towers that possessed only an average lean, past the lights of cafés and restaurants that discharged heavy aromas of pastry, garlic, coffee and grilled fish; and all the time, from the canals, the sea water and the sewage, came the lingering, distinctive scent of the city.

Fortuny's words, which had riled Lucy more and more as the day had progressed, were still with her. And as she stared into the glow of the passing shop windows she felt—for the first time since leaving home a month earlier—quite alone. Empty. An emptiness made all the more oppressive by the very time of day, that uncertain hour between six and seven. The suicide hour. At least, that was Lucy's name for it. Perhaps, she wondered, this was why there were aperitif hours, cocktail hours, the hour in the pub after work when little rituals—the tinkle of glasses, the chatter within—occupied the mind so that nobody would notice the hopes of the day collapsing in on themselves and shivering beneath the rim of the horizon as night rolled in. Suddenly she was in need of human company, missed the family—once always something of a world unto itself—and the few friends she'd made at school.

As well as Marco, she had made some friends at the music college and they had already gone out together a couple of times. But it was Marco to whom her thoughts turned when the need of company was upon her, as it was now. The thrill of her arrival in the city having subsided, she looked about a small square, acknowledging that she was indeed utterly alone. She also realised that her loneliness was of a different kind than any she'd experienced before, the sense of emptiness beyond tears. There was no sense of a place called 'home' that she could fall back on, even yearn for. Nothing like that, just this unbearable hour, just the day. And so she ambled on, vaguely looked out for a telephone from which she might call her father, but dismissed the thought after a quick calculation told her it was four in the morning in Australia.

Closer to San Marco the streets were still surprisingly uncrowded. The tourist season had not yet started in earnest and the people passing by or gazing into the shop windows seemed to be mostly families and couples, closed units unto themselves, some of whom occasionally paused to glance at the young woman in the long, navy blue coat, before moving on to their various destinations.

The gloomy thought passed through her that her first excursion from home was doomed to come to nothing; that she was just another silly little thing fooling herself with grand ideas, like every other foolish little thing who had ever existed down through the years. The bars were full, there was laughter in the air, but it was the excluding laughter of old friends. This was no city in which to carry gloomy thoughts around. Only the day before, hadn't Marco said that the city was an island and its people lived like islands, each in their closed, tight circles? She could have stopped for a small glass of wine in one of those bars, but at that moment having a drink on her own held no appeal.

She crossed a series of tiny bridges, over canals now calm with the completion of the day's commerce, until her chosen path opened out onto the main square of the city. There was a string quartet, some of them students from the Conservatorium, playing at the front of a café (she too would soon be playing there, with Marco, who had suggested it), but she only vaguely knew these students. She walked quickly, between the two columns of St Mark and St Theodore, to the waterfront of the Grand Canal and onto the Riva Schiavoni, along which Fortuny had strolled in his white summer suit only a few hours before. The music of the café orchestras followed her, faintly. Soon enough she would herself be seated on the Piazza San Marco, providing incidental music to French, German and Japanese tourists, but not with the cello. Her jazz piano was always going to come in handy and she would be condemned to the theme from *The Godfather*. And, perhaps, that was all she was good for after all.

A vaporetto was waiting to cross to Giudecca. She paused, undecided, then jumped on at the last moment, the glow of the evening sky on the wide dome of the Salute the most miserable thing she'd ever seen. It was a short trip and she stood at the entrance to the boat, watching the waves smack against its edge and taking in the invigorating breeze off the open waters. On Giudecca she strolled to Marco's small flat, rang his bell twice, but it was later than she'd thought and he wasn't in. He would, more than likely, be at one of the bars in Cannaregio where they played jazz.

On the ride back she hunched her shoulders and pushed her hands deep into her pockets, determined to practise more that evening—and the next morning, and in the afternoon. Determined to prove Fortuny, or anybody else, wrong. A water taxi passed and rocked the vaporetto slightly. Lucy leaned back in her seat, lost in her thoughts, and as she leaned back, Molly's voice came whispering back through the years: 'Can you play? Why, you're an *artist*!' Molly had breathed the word as if she had been standing in some vast cathedral rather than a suburban garden. 'An artist.'

And as soon as Molly had breathed the word into her life, the world of the artist, that whole world of the elect, had unrolled before Lucy, the most enchanting of myths, the most alluring of landscapes where mountains poked up through clouds and mist towards a vast, blue sky stretching out forever. And standing on a craggy rock, a dark, commanding figure overseeing the whole spectacle as if watching its birth. Watching as if having summoned the spectacle, created it. For, in Lucy's mind, from that moment on, the artist would always be a kind of god, who stood on mountain peaks and brought whole worlds to life that had never previously existed.

Amid the swirling soup of worlds coming to life, the artist stood still, accountable to no one. Not even thinking, because the whole process, Lucy imagined, took you way beyond mere thinking, into the terrain of pure, unerring instinct. And it was her own instinct that she would always defer to, that would never, she felt sure, let her down. And it never had—at least, not until tonight, when she had begun for the first time to doubt the whole religion of her instinct. But she was condemned to pursue it, this world of the elect. Penniless, or even slum born, artists were the true aristocrats of the world. And from the moment Molly had breathed that world into their suburban garden, Lucy had known there would be no other world for her. It was that, or nothing.

Later that night, hers the only light shining in the quiet lane she lived in, Lucy wrote to her father. So that he might visualise her surroundings, she described in detail the view from the tiny study in which she wrote, the yellow and orange rendered houses now silver under the streetlight, the awnings, the tiny terraces, the pot plants, the dull light on the inky canal, and the slippery moss green of the tide line on the bricks. It was her third letter home and she spoke of Fortuny for the first time, of the kindness of the Maestro in even agreeing to see her, and the invaluable nature of the lessons she would receive. That done, she scribbled postcards to her old schoolfriends, Helena Applegate and Sally Happer.

One letter, two postcards, three people. Didn't seem much. What did it matter? At school everybody had gangs, gangs of friends, they called them, who sat around at lunchtime having conversations about the number of telephones in their houses, and the one who had the most telephones won the conversation. They counted friends, she mused, like they counted the household telephones. And so, when Lucy had refused to join their gangs, they'd called her a snob. One letter, two postcards. Not much, but enough, she thought.

When Lucy finally lay back in the narrow single bed and closed her eyes, she revisited the morning in her mind's eye. She once more visualised Fortuny's salon, its hand-made fabrics and cluttered walls, until it became the secret chamber through which she passed in her dreams.

PART THREE

Chapter Seven

THE couch was covered in cushions. It was long, and there were possibly twenty to thirty differently shaped and coloured cushions artfully arranged on it. Fortuny had asked Lucy to sit, but the couch didn't have the look of a couch that is sat upon, so she chose instead the chair beside it.

It was a bright, sunny Tuesday morning. The light seeped into the heavy glass, into the repeated circular patterns, of Fortuny's windows, but didn't seem to penetrate them. The room remained only partially lit and Lucy noticed that a lamp had been switched on near the cello. There was no sense of the courtyard below, or the garden. Fortuny's house was a closed world, as if cut off from the life outside or the progress of time. The couch, the walls, the whole salon was cluttered with artefacts in the Venetian style, but it was also, it now seemed to Lucy, a room designed to leave the observer in no doubt that the occupant of the house had lived a full and rich life; a room like a living scrap book or picture album. She was intoxicated by the surroundings.

'The time is convenient for you?'

Lucy turned to Fortuny. 'Yes. Of course it is.'

'Good. It cannot be changed anyway.' He reached for a few pages of yellowed sheet music. 'I thought we could start with this. It is an exercise, but it shouldn't be underestimated.'

This time there was no small talk and Fortuny handed Lucy the sheets to a piece of music she hadn't played in years. It was, indeed, a student exercise and she walked slowly to the cello, disappointed with the task she'd been given.

But playing the exercise was even more dispiriting. It made her feel as if she were a pupil of sixteen or seventeen again, and she wondered if this was the reason she had been given it, to put her in her place once more. She even wondered if he had agreed to teach her out of a sardonic desire to belittle her, to teach her lessons other than musical. She suddenly wondered, with a feeling of apprehension, whether even the lessons of Signor Bellini might be more valuable than those of Fortuny, but quickly dispelled the thought.

She felt sure that her execution of the exercise was flat and passionless, yet when she had finished it and turned to Fortuny he praised her technique, made only brief criticisms here and there, and finished with a few minor suggestions.

He asked her to play it again and she returned to the music, her spirits suddenly lifted. This was no longer just some student exercise that was almost humiliating to have to play in front of a maestro but a work of genuine stature, to be taken seriously and treated with utmost respect.

Again, when she had finished, Fortuny made only minor observations, suggesting small adjustments to her technique and posture and, overall, seemed quite pleased with the work of his new student.

But there was one small point, Fortuny said, and here he asked Lucy to repeat the most difficult section of the piece, one that required a rapid succession of notes and which, admittedly, Lucy had always found testing. She obliged, repeating the phrase, and when she had finished Fortuny leaned forward, smiling.

'No, not like that.'

Suddenly his hands were enfolding hers and he was slowly guiding her thumb behind the fingerboard.

'The thumb slides back, like so, and this finger follows naturally. Then you flick the string with your finger, not the bow. You see?'

He guided her hand once more, still smiling. Then she tried it herself, and a movement that had always been a difficult rush of notes suddenly fell effortlessly into place. She played it again, and again. The same phrase. She looked up, grinning. Fortuny nodded approvingly.

'It is, I believe, what the Americans call—' here Fortuny broke from the Italian in which they usually conversed and said in awkward English '—a neat trick.'

Lucy didn't reply but, instead, played the piece again, then stopped, looking down at the fingerboard of the cello, marvelling at the simplicity of it all.

Fortuny eased back in his seat, clearly enjoying himself, or so it seemed to Lucy. And he was. She couldn't know that until her lessons began it had been over a year since Fortuny had listened to the work of a student. A year since a cello had last been played in the salon and its many rooms had registered its music. Outwardly, he remained calm, the maestro in charge of the lesson. Inwardly, he thrilled to the sound. The previous week he had felt the necessity to be stern, but now he relaxed and let the music pass over him.

By the time the lesson was over and she had gone down into Fortuny's courtyard, Lucy felt transformed. The sunshine that had meant nothing earlier that morning now seemed to signify the advent of wonderful things; warmed her like heated brandy. The long, arduous hours of practice, the years of work, the doubting, the endless preparation had, she now believed, been worthwhile after all, and she would one day sit at the table of serious artists and be taken as their equal. And, of course—whatever misgivings she may have felt about Fortuny's teaching now dissolved—he was indubitably the Maestro, his lessons inspiring.

Fortuny, who had smiled and shaken her hand as she'd left, sat in his armchair in the salon. He remained there for a considerable time, quite still, staring at the light reflected on the windows and breathing in the last, lingering notes of the music and the perfume of the young woman who had just left. At last he rose and lightly brushed the cello strings with his fingers before calling Rosa to bring coffee into the courtyard.

The old cello stood under the lamps of the room like a well-polished exhibit, and as he glanced at it Fortuny remembered the end of things: recalled how the universe of his youth had acquired boundaries, relived the end of his career. His entire life had been music and he could not forget how the music had begun leaving him, sending its telltale signs to his fingers and ears.

At first only he had noticed. At sixty, just as he had begun to believe himself to be invulnerable, the talent that for so many years he had taken for granted began to announce its departure. Slyly, almost strategically, like a lover quietly leaving the former object of his adoration, age was signalling the endgame, ushering in its inevitable outcome: silent rooms and quietened halls, waiting to be vacated and filled with the sound of other people's lives, other people's music. For the music that had once rushed to him was ebbing, the power that it gave declining.

In the past, the concerts, the dinners, the parties, the women had been all that he had ever yearned for, but gradually, with time, every performance had become an endurance and a test. Instead of hungrily anticipating the flourishes, the intricacies of concert play that only a few ever achieved, he secretly came to dread them. Each concert became a potential date to circle in his diary and mark the day, the precise hour, even the minute, when Fortuny would finally lose it.

During this time his temper became shorter, he felt more vulnerable. He became a burden to his friends— and to himself. And when he imagined the concert hall he no longer conceived of a triumphant scene but one of potential demise and humiliation.

He had performed in public for the last time the previous year, at the age of sixty-one. He was far from being an old man, and many argued that it was much too soon, implored him to continue. Fortuny convinced them that it was precisely the right moment, without ever saying why. What he did say—handing on a line that had been passed on to him years before by a retiring master—was that it was best to retire while people were still asking 'Why did you?' rather than 'Why *don't* you?'

The facility, the gift of that little bit extra, had finally departed. The separation was complete. He had announced his retirement and had not performed in public since.

Now, waiting for his coffee in the courtyard, he sat in the spring sunshine, contemplating the lilacs, the hydrangeas and the creeping vines over the wall. The young woman's music seemed to inhabit the garden, cascading over the garden walls like the jasmine and lingering in the air like the scent of the flower. In the near distance he could hear a passing taxi and vaguely discern its wake as water smacked against the edges of his canal. Out at sea, a deep green wave of music rolled towards the islands of the city with the inexorability of all tides, rolling green through the days and grey through the silent nights. Fortuny leaned back in his chair, closing his eyes, as if already anticipating its advent, his sixty-two-year-old heart preparing for the imagined moment of its arrest.

Later, back in his salon, Fortuny thought once more of Lucy. That mixture of fascination and unease he had felt at their first encounter had never quite left him. But he knew her now, or was beginning to. And she would, he reflected, be pleasant company. Engaging, even amusing. Fresh. And what she lacked in refinement, she made up for with…what? Energy, he supposed. For, to what he increasingly felt was his tired, old world, she brought a spark. A touch of electricity. But exactly what she would spark into life was yet to be established. Still, something was better than nothing.

Fortuny sipped his brandy as he strolled across to the Venus on the wall, pausing in front of it. But as he stared at it, something disturbed his calm, like the sudden awareness of children rushing through brittle, fallen park leaves disturbing the stillness of an afternoon walk. He stood motionless in front of the painting. What was it? A gesture, the hand of the Venus, the wrist? Perhaps the eyes, or the smile… Fortuny had possessed the painting for almost thirty years but, inconceivably, it now seemed that something had always escaped his attention, something he was only now beginning to notice but couldn't pinpoint. Either that, or the painting had altered.

Then it occurred to Fortuny that it was he himself who had altered, and, accordingly, so had his perceptions. Certainly, there was now something in the painting that he had never noticed before. He was alarmed and turned away, almost frightened to look back.

A gesture, an expression? But what *was* it? Somewhere within him a thought threatened to burst into life and Fortuny crushed the bloom. But it returned again and again, until he slowly turned back to the painting and simply allowed the thought to be. And while he was staring at the familiar face of the standing Venus, he suddenly remembered Lucy's eyes, which often stared directly ahead when she'd finished playing. He studied the broad forehead, the sweet skin and the long, flowing hair of Venus, and slapped his thighs, reproving himself for not having noticed the resemblance till now. Until that moment, Lucy had held the promise of pleasant company, was even common to look at from certain angles and would surely be a social embarrassment.

But the girl had clearly entered the painting, and he was suddenly possessed by an inescapable belief that whenever he looked at it from now on he would see her, this Lucy, and not one of those modern young creatures capable of dismantling you even as they desired you.

He slumped into his armchair, downed his brandy in one throw, as he always had when young, and stared at the moving pigments of the painting, at the figure emerging from the shell, as if she were about to approach him.

She couldn't dispel the touch of his fingers. In order to demonstrate the intricacies of that 'neat trick' he'd had to hold her hand in his. And although he had remained perfectly at ease, almost clinical (as, indeed, her father would handle a patient), the combination of touch, sight and the scent of Fortuny's freshly shaven face had been spellbinding, even though she couldn't possibly have acknowledged the sensation at the time. She couldn't have spoken, she knew. So she played, again and again, exploring the neat trick that he had passed on to her. And now, sitting in her kitchen, the door open to the afternoon sunshine, she relived his touch.

A lesson was only a lesson after all. And lessons were important. And if he touched her hand, if he guided her fingers, it was all part of his teaching. She saw him again, standing behind her, leaning over her, guiding her tanned arms as if holding the bow and finger board, and Lucy the cello itself and not the cello player. Her hands, her fingers, gold in the grey morning, yawned, stretched over the strings, arched over the finger board and slid down the neck of the instrument, William Hills & Co., 1893. And if she felt the shadow of his breath passing over her shoulders, faintly flavoured with garlic and the whiff of tobacco, it was all part of the lesson.

All the time the music seemed to be playing itself. They were filling the emptiness of a spare hour in the middle of the afternoon with a music lesson. And if his fingers should move slowly along her arms and gradually come to rest on her shoulders, her neck…to trace the lines of bone, sinew and growing muscle under the skin, that would be part of the lesson too. Then the music would stop, the lesson would stop, and she would know why she was there.

First touch could do all that. And she knew instantly that the hands, the fingers of Fortuny, had known the world in ways that she could both imagine and not imagine. She remembered being fifteen, sixteen all over again, when everything had turned to sex. And everybody, all her girlfriends at school (the extraordinarily mature Helena, whose perfect legs could stop the school, the shy Sally Happer from the country, who was bullied with sarcasm and whom Lucy took under her wing, silencing the mob) talked constantly of it. A nod, a glance, a telephone number. It was all sex. And every day she could feel her own body swelling and growing, watched it; every morning more of it. Then came the stares in the street, or anywhere, the stares she ached for, welcomed—and the revulsion at being leered over.

Six months after Molly died, the question of what to do with it all was answered. It was one late winter morning in her final year at school, during a recital at the university, when she met a third-year music student with a violin. He'd looked up at her backstage just before performing and grinned at her, a forbidden cigarette wedged in his teeth. No nerves, as if everything were a giant lark and music had been invented for fun. He was five years older than she, and he knew what to do. After a few months he left for London, and although he promised to write, the letters were few and far between. Then his last letter arrived, a brief communication letting her know that 'everything seemed so different over here'. She was sad for a short while. But she was seventeen, and a wise man in a book had told her that the emotions of the young are violent, but not durable. The wise man was right, and by the time summer came the sadness had passed and she immersed herself in the sanctuary of Fortuny's music, to which she always turned when the world had let her down. There were other young men after that, but she'd learnt not to go in too deep. Fortuny's world called and she would always be leaving.

When she arrived the next week Lucy played a far more difficult piece, one she had been instructed to rehearse at the previous lesson. When Fortuny spoke, he offered quite a number of suggestions, but once more they were only minor and he made them with the utmost consideration. He was, she eventually concluded, almost being charming.

When she'd finished she sat listening to him, nodding at appropriate moments and appreciating the extraordinary detail of his comments. She also noticed, once again, the musical resonance of his voice. Musical in the sense that it was a note: an A below middle C, or thereabouts. His initial bullying was completely gone from his manner now. He had become a reassuring figure and she would no longer treat the lessons as a weekly test. Sitting on the practice stool, Lucy felt relaxed, even casually played a phrase of music briefly, then remarked on the enjoyment she gained from their lessons.

He said nothing, and she noted how straight his back was as he sat in the chair, noted the self-absorption as he stared at the wall hangings in silence, and began to feel that she had overstayed her time. The silence continued and she was on the point of picking up her bag and dismissing herself when he finally spoke.

'Will you accompany me to the opera on Saturday?'

Lucy sat perfectly still, almost closed her eyes as, outwardly calm, she registered the import of the words. Fortuny passed a tired hand through his hair and continued.

'But, of course, if that is inconvenient—'

'No. No, it's not,' she said in a rush.

'Then it would give me pleasure.' Fortuny's voice hummed on the brink of continuing, but Lucy got in first.

'Yes, I'd like to.'

Once more silence followed their brief dialogue, and Lucy looked around the salon for the umpteenth time; looked from the artefacts to the paintings, to astute copies of paintings—Giorgione, Modigliani, Matisse— at the expanse of the salon itself, wondering at the society she seemed to be entering. At home she'd mixed with what her father, who never attended extended family functions, called the 'nobs'—that glittering bunch of brazen new money, and the actors and politicians keen to have some of the glitter rub off on them. She was familiar enough with that world, but not this one, the door to which Fortuny had just opened. This world came with the whole, private mythology that had sustained her through her late teens and which drove her now.

Her gaze returned to rest on Fortuny. Throughout her adolescence and beyond she had studied him day and night. Now she conversed with him simply, mat-ter-of-factly as, she told herself, one artist would con-verse with another, the maestro and the maestro's apprentice. And, together, they would now enter that rich, exciting society she'd always imagined to be part of his world, and hers. The prospect was at once in-toxicating and terrifying. She hoped that he would not ask her to play again because she was sure that she would never be able to control the shaking of her hands. And that was the last thing she wanted Fortuny to see, for then he might reconsider his choice of com-panion, might even withdraw his invitation.

For Fortuny, it had been a decisive moment. The young woman could have refused him, found the offer silly, even laughed and rendered him ridiculous. And at this point of his life Fortuny feared humiliation above all other experiences. But she had accepted his offer, simply, matter-of-factly, like—he quickly re-minded himself, remembering the way it had always been—any desirable young woman accepting a gen-tleman's proposal for a social engagement. But the calmness of his features was superficial, and he knew it. For here she was, one of those frightening young mermaids, and whatever she might think of him, For-tuny had acquired, during this first year of retire-ment—retirement not only from music but from the world he'd known—more than a little of Signor Pruf-rock. As much as he had called these modern young creatures with his eyes, he was, in his newly acquired insecurity, petrified at the thought of what on earth he would do if one were to return his call with a simple 'Yes, I'd like to', and Signor Prufrock were to meet his mermaid after all.

Then, with one hand resting on the arm of his chair, Fortuny casually gestured towards the cello and suggested she play again. Lucy froze.

'The same?' she asked, but Fortuny shook his head and gently insisted that it wasn't a lesson. The lesson was over for the day.

'For the pleasure of listening,' he replied. 'Whatever you wish.'

She paused for a moment, then turned nervously to the cello again. But his words, and the calmness of his manner, were soothing and her anxieties disappeared as she began to play, her hands steady after all. Fortuny closed his eyes, his head resting against the back of his chair, his fingers lightly tapping its sides, sometimes seeming even to conduct as he anticipated the flurries and pauses, the light and shade of the work.

And in what was neither a performance nor a lesson, Lucy felt herself entering the still point of the music. The tips of her fingers, her lips, her arms moved as one, while the rest of her sat perfectly still. She became an observer of her own playing, watching, as if disembodied, an unfamiliar young woman playing as if suddenly blessed with a great gift. The gift, passing through her like a ghost, indifferent and transitory.

But when the piece ended the feeling left her. Lucy looked up from the cello like a dreamer, like the young girl who had played night after night throughout the last years of her schooling so that she might forget for a time her guilt and her sadness. Her eyes now opening to the room about her, the dream world faded, leaving only nostalgia for its protective presence, and the vague, gathering understanding that that was how inspiration worked. You were there, and you weren't there, just like those nights when she'd played to obliterate her pain. And as the memory passed through her, so too did the thought that she had, all those years ago, been blessed with that pain, for it had introduced her to the world of inspired oblivion.

Fortuny opened his eyes, smiling, nodding. 'Bravo,' he whispered.

Lucy sat, trancelike, thrilling to the secret thought that she might really be different after all. That here, in Fortuny's house, in the dim light of the salon, the gift that had always been there could finally be summoned. She sat, saying nothing, only rehearsing over and over again the words she would say to Fortuny. Is it there? Do you see it in me? But she would never ask, for if it were true the asking would surely be unnecessary, and she was left only with the anxiety of wondering. Fortuny, in his chair, was impassive.

He saw her to the door, then smiled graciously, shook her hand, and watched as she descended into the courtyard.

Walking back, counting out her long strides, Lucy dwelt on Fortuny's words, the ease with which he had asked her to accompany him to the opera, the nonchalance of her reply. The cello. The music. The house she had never thought to see, let alone become an accepted part of. And now she was. Hadn't Fortuny asked her to play simply for the pleasure of listening? And hadn't Lucy played the way she'd always known she could? Fantastic as it might have seemed, the two halves of her world had finally closed on each other. And there, in mid-stride, in a small Venetian square near a low canal, Lucy heard the click she'd waited for all her life.

She suddenly stopped, utterly still, her eyes wide and barely registering the glassed conservatory to her immediate left in which a man was currently reading, the flaking buildings about her or the little motorboats on the canal. The shrubbery, unruffled by any wind, the entire scene was as still as Lucy herself. Crystalline, perfect and complete. A hard-etched moment that no amount of time could wash away, that would forever be a part of her. She was Lucy McBride and, from now on, nothing and no one could touch her. She had landed, and she knew it.

* * *

The lessons with Signor Bellini continued. He was an attentive teacher, and a tolerant one. Demanding when it was needed, but clinical. The passion rose in his voice, it seemed, only when he spoke of the small vineyard he kept with his brothers on a little property just outside Treviso. He even promised to bring her a bottle of his wine, but never did.

She didn't tell him of her meetings with Fortuny. Perhaps he would find out in time. But he was a discreet man, for whom business was business, and no doubt would never mention it if he did.

Towards the end of the week, another letter arrived from her father. A cold front had passed through the city the week before and everybody was wearing overcoats. An unusually heavy fall of winter rain had swollen the river till it had broken, flooded and lapped around the steps of the boathouses along its banks. The tram that had once brought her back home at night was less of an event now that he knew she would not be stepping off it and crossing the wide, open street with her long strides. But he liked the sound of her flat. He had, by the way, just finished reading Ruskin's *The Stones of Venice*. It was pretty good, really. She should give it a go. Did she realise that John Ruskin had lived at the Hotel Danieli while writing it?

Alone in her flat, Lucy laughed fondly at her father's words, at his tone, which was that of the pedantic amateur scholar, the trace of his irony audible on the page. No, she hadn't realised that, but checked it in one her guide books and discovered that her father was right, of course. He was always right. She smiled at the thought, and it was then that she remembered *his* brave smile on the day she had left for Italy: a brave smile that had acknowledged the final scattering of the small family that had been a world unto itself, a world enough to sustain them all for so long now gone, flown into the wider world, and beyond.

Before she fell asleep, Lucy wrote a quick reply, skipping the dull spots of her time so far, judging that he wouldn't want to know. Instead, she spoke again of the school, of Signor Fortuny's lessons, his kindness and, finally, his recent invitation to her.

Clothes were not something that concerned Lucy. At least, not the way they had always concerned the girls at her school who, when they weren't teasing the Sally Happers of this world, talked endlessly about fashion and pop songs. And when they weren't doing that they were talking about sex, of course—and love. But not love in the sense that meant anything to Lucy. When these girls talked about love they meant marriage to men of appropriate class and sufficient substance to receive the investment of their beauty. For many of them, their beauty would remain their most valuable asset, and from a very early age their lives were directed

to making just the right investment. To Lucy there was
something depressingly banal about going through life
looking for somebody to fall in love with in this cal-
culated way, but this was what they did. And when
they met that somebody, they would marry them, the
rest would follow, and their lives would be complete.
It was not so much an act of love as an exchange of
goods (this was more Sally Happer's sentiment than
Lucy's, but Lucy agreed). And the goods always had to
look their best, and to look their best they had to be
draped in the latest fashion.

So love and fashion merged, the one needing the
other as a gift needed its wrapping. Lucy had always
believed she had been born decades too late. She displayed a disdain for fashion and—except for those
nifty and durable tunes of the 1930s and '40s—wasn't
the slightest bit interested in the pop music that came
and went and which everybody sang for a day or two.
Clothes, the love that led only to a suburban marriage, pop songs. It was all the same. These things did
not concern her.

And so, when she looked for something special to
wear to the opera, to wear for Fortuny, she realised she
didn't really have the 'right' outfit. So be it. Why should
she? She would go with what she had, a simple dress
that she usually wore on the rare occasions when she
went 'out'. Besides, the whole idea of standing in front
of a mirror, wrestling with the absurd question of what

to wear, was an activity of lesser creatures, those creatures who went through life looking for someone to fall
in love with. No, clothes didn't concern her, she told
herself—but she told herself in a voice that only half
convinced her and to which she was only half listening.

Chapter Eight

IT WAS a society unto itself, this opera circle, as overwhelming as the perfumes that surrounded her. Lucy, plunged into the thick of such affluence, was dazzled by the chic clothes that she had always told herself were the banal concern of the superficial and of no interest to her. She felt instantly drab, and when Fortuny introduced her to a small group of people she nodded with each introduction, said nothing, and was relieved when she was ignored.

Fortuny and his little band chatted from within that self-enclosed world of long familiarity that greeted newcomers as intruders, which at least left Lucy free to observe. Part of her was fascinated by the spectacle, part of her just wanted to be gone, to be shot of the place, like an impostor who might at any moment be exposed.

They were there for *Madama Butterfly*. Some of the crowd wore Japanese-style outfits, some occasionally waved fans; the rest simply exuded wealth. They had all gone to great trouble, there was a real sense of occasion, and Lucy, although no stranger to the fashionable at home, was mixing with an unfamiliar tribe here. The informality of her country's ways, the easy manner which she'd always prided herself on possessing, now made her feel awkward and conspicuous and wish herself invisible. When the buzzers at last signalled the beginning of the performance she was happy to disappear into the darkness.

Afterwards, standing in the foyer, she turned her attention back to the small circle of Fortuny's friends. From time to time, Fortuny turned to her, asking what she thought of this or that aspect of the performance, and although there were considered pauses after she voiced her approval of the tenor who sang Pinkerton, or her reservations about the soprano in the title role, the conversation always closed in on itself and she was left once again to observe—and was content to do so.

Perhaps, she mused, these people were merely acquaintances. Did the Fortunys of this world have real friends? she wondered. This group didn't look or sound like friends but, rather, had the air of eternal hangers-on. Name-droppers in search of names to drop, hunters and gatherers of anecdote, of gossip, of tales to colour their conversation pieces when required. She'd met their type before. Oh, they were more posh than the home-grown variety, but they were the same all right, or so they seemed to her. They had given Lucy the cold shoulder, presumably, she thought, because she wasn't sufficiently 'dressed' for the occasion, that she was 'plain' on the outside and therefore must be 'plain' on the inside. In the face of such shallow triviality, she felt free to pass judgement on them. But perhaps she was being unfair? Perhaps on another night they might appear the most entertaining and amiable of people. But tonight she was in no mood to be generous, to give these hangers-on the benefit of the doubt. Then she realised that she might just be sulking, that it might be obvious to everyone, and with an effort she composed herself and wiped the look from her face.

Moments later, Fortuny clapped his hands together, signifying that the evening was concluded and, gauging that they had seen enough society for one evening, suggested in an aside to Lucy that she accompany him back to his house. He spoke in an almost conspiratorial manner, the way the famous give hangers-on the slip, and it was done with such speed and aplomb that Lucy was left in no doubt that he had performed such exits all his life.

On the brief walk back from the theatre, they talked about the story of the opera. Fortuny told Lucy about the young nineteenth-century American writer whose tale had provided Puccini and his librettists with their material. And when Lucy said that she thought the tragedy was a bit of a melodrama, Fortuny smiled without commenting, a smile that seemed to say, Youth.

Yes, youth would say that. But not once during the walk back (and Lucy only realised this afterwards) did they talk about the music.

At Fortuny's, they at first ignored the salon where Rosa had left a tray of wafer biscuits and a carafe of white wine, and ascended the steps to the *portego* on the *piano nobile*. Fortuny dismissed Rosa and ushered Lucy along the *portego*, which was lined with family portraits and Venetian street scenes over various periods in history. He talked as they went but Lucy, who hadn't seen the room before, only half heard his commentary on the surrounding objects, the paintings, the marble busts and furniture that claimed her attention. Although the night had become chilly, he opened the doors and they stepped outside.

Lucy found herself facing that section of the Grand Canal that flowed under the Accademia bridge, that large wooden bridge she had crossed so many times. It was visible in the distance but the view she was used to was now reversed and she felt that, if she looked hard enough, she might even see herself crossing over the previous week, staring at the many closed, magnificent houses that lined the canal and wondering what the view was like from their balconies. The lights of restaurants, cafés and private houses delineated the edges of the canal and cast their beams onto the waters, their golden shards of light broken occasionally by late-night vaporetti.

It was too chilly to stay long outside and Fortuny suggested they return to the salon where their refreshments waited for them. The wine, Lucy noted with surprise, was the same inexpensive wine she had tasted in the little bars and osterias around the city—not bad wine, but nothing special as she had expected. She told herself she shouldn't be surprised, and decided that, consistent with the idiosyncrasies of the very rich, Fortuny must actually prefer it. In fact, it was his favourite, a standard table wine from the nearby region of Friuli, which Rosa bought every week from a small osteria in a tiny lane at the back of San Marco.

The glass she drank from, on the other hand, was a work of art, its deep swirls of blue and green like the waves she had immersed herself in every summer of her youth. Vaguely remembering the aphorism—a framed poster—that had hung on her wall as a teenager, she asked herself, are you drinking the water or the wave? She had never understood its meaning then and she didn't now, but it seemed somehow appropriate to be asking herself the question again. She handled the glass carefully, replaced it on the table with deliberation and care.

They sipped their drinks in silence for a while, then Fortuny spoke.

'I am invited to many of these engagements, but I find it dull to go to them alone,' he said, tactfully forgetting his old friend Carla.

Lucy nodded, already understanding the implication, but said nothing. She watched Fortuny, who ran his fingers around the edges of his glass then spoke softly, in a low, almost guttural whisper that carried the charcoal edge of a lifetime smoker.

'Would you care to be my companion on these occasions?'

In the half-light of the salon, Lucy stared back at him, aware of conflicting responses to the question. On the one hand, it was indeed an intimidating society to which he was now opening the door for her. On the other hand, she was not one to be easily intimidated by anyone, and this was, after all, Fortuny's world she was being invited to share. She would be his companion, and he would introduce her to his world. She had also sensed in him a trace of uncertainty, even insecurity, as he'd asked her, and her immediate instinct was a desire to reassure him. And while it made Fortuny appear all the more human and approachable, even vulnerable, there was also something poignant about this which, she fancifully noted, made her impulse to please seem like wanting to comfort an anxious god.

'Just to these engagements, you understand,' he added by way of explanation, and continued, without allowing an awkward pause to intrude, 'but you, no doubt, have many friends. You go out frequently and don't have time. That is understandable.'

He put down his glass of wine and clapped his hands together as if the matter were now closed, indeed, had never been mentioned, and Lucy spoke.

'I'd like that.'

Fortuny turned to her, clearly surprised, then picked up his glass and sipped from it before slowly nodding at her without further comment. He poured her more wine, rose to his feet, and the two walked about the salon. Lucy had, of course, seen the copy of the *Birth of Venus* and now Fortuny told her about many of the other paintings on the walls, the artists and their subjects. When they came to a halt in front of the reclining figure of a naked woman, Lucy recognised it as a Munch. Struck by the likeness to the original, she turned to Fortuny, commenting on the artist's skill, and asked who he was.

At first Fortuny just stared at her, and when Lucy repeated the question looked bemused.

'Munch,' he said.

'Yes,' Lucy continued, 'but who painted it?'

He frowned slightly then finally registered her meaning. 'Munch,' he repeated. 'It's not a copy, Munch painted it. The Botticelli is the only replica in the room.'

Lucy blushed. She had, she knew, insulted Fortuny. She had simply assumed that this was a room decorated solely with the works of second-rate artists, friends, and only copies of famous paintings. But here too, as in the historical arena, public names were private possessions. And as she slowly swung round in a circle, taking in the room again, she saw the bold, bright colours of a Matisse on the back wall, and what was unmistakably a Renoir not far from it. When her eyes finally returned to Fortuny he was taking the Munch down from the wall.

'I knew him,' he said quietly, turning the painting over. 'Forget the painting for the moment. Look at the painter.' There was no hint of pretension or condescension in his voice.

He passed the painting, face down, across to Lucy who examined the back of it, unsure of what she was meant to be looking at. Then, written in pencil, she saw a column of figures, a line ruled across them at the bottom and a total circled. She studied the numbers then looked up at Fortuny.

'It's the money for his physician. Munch was consumptive,' he said quietly. 'He added up the sum total of his debts on the back of a beautiful painting.' Almost ashamed, he added, 'I bought it from him just after the war. It was the only time I ever met him. I didn't pay much. I should have paid more.'

He replaced the picture back on the wall, taking care that it should be level, and returned to his wine. It was as though he'd forgotten about her for the time being and was giving private thanks to the painter for the painting. Lucy stared about the room once again. Not for the first time since arriving, she felt like a bungling colonial.

It was then that Fortuny explained about his grandfather, told her how he had studied with Braque in Paris then ditched his creative aspirations to embark on a very lucrative career as an art dealer. He explained how Eduardo Fortuny had possessed an unerring eye for the real thing, and how much of the present collection was testimony to his talent. And when Fortuny, his grandson, now spoke of the real thing it was almost with a religious conviction that made it quite obvious he would have nothing to do with any newfangled ideas about democracy and art. Art, his tone made it perfectly clear, was not democratic, and never had been. It was a belief which, like any article of faith, was beyond questioning. One either believed, or one didn't.

Then, for the first time, he spoke briefly about his family's history, dwelling on its more exalted moments, carefully omitting to mention the branch that was stationed in the Aegean and had once gone to war with a neighbouring island over a donkey.

Soon after, Lucy took her coat and left. Fortuny offered her a taxi but she wanted to think, and as she did her best thinking on her feet, she declined the offer and waved from the courtyard as he closed the door.

Walking back to her flat, Lucy forgot her indiscretion and imagined, instead, Fortuny, seated in the same armchair in which she had left him, his drink untouched by his side, staring into space and listening to the room. But the face she carried with her from the evening was Fortuny the Younger, the face she'd first seen on the record sleeve years before. Not that there was much difference between Fortuny then and Fortuny now. Time had done little to alter his features. The image she'd become infatuated with and the man she'd accompanied to the opera were not, she told herself, much different in appearance. His hair was now silver grey, but nothing more. The moody, solemn stare was still there, only now he, *her* Fortuny, had acquired the third dimension that the photograph had lacked. And this three-dimensional Fortuny had asked her, with, she felt sure, a touching hint of insecurity that she might say no, to be his companion. If only— and here she allowed herself a slight smile—if only he knew.

Her feet passed lightly over the stones of the city. In spite of the cold she paused, breathed deeply and smiled to herself. The lights were still burning in restaurants and cafés, but there were no boats now and no sounds, only Lucy's footsteps ringing in the night. She had passed through the eye of a needle. She was there. In Fortuny's world.

At the end of a lesson a week later, Fortuny mentioned that he would like to buy her a gift, a small token, he said, of his appreciation. He had said this with a casualness that implied that neither a 'yes' nor a 'no' was of any consequence—a surprising characteristic that she was beginning to recognise as more defence than indifference. And as much as she protested that a gift wasn't necessary, that the time she spent in his company was reward enough, he insisted that it would give him great pleasure.

And so, a few hours later, puzzled but flattered, Lucy found herself in one of the more opulent fashion shops of this fashion-obsessed city. She'd looked in the windows of this particular place on the few occasions she'd passed it, wondering what sort of women could afford to throw their money around on clothes like this. Now, suddenly, despite her repeated protests, which Fortuny had met with the most imploring of looks, she found herself inside.

Fortuny sat in a small armchair while Lucy stood in the middle of the showroom with Signora Giovanna, the owner of the salon, who was fussing over a long evening dress. It had nothing as vulgar as a price tag attached to it and had clearly been made for one of the few women in the world who could afford to buy it. Lucy had turned once, twice, and was turning a third time for the benefit of Fortuny, when he finally shook his head. He then launched into a long discussion about colour and cut with the proprietress, a plainly but elegantly dressed middle-aged woman. They ignored Lucy, and when she suggested that he couldn't be serious about buying the dress, or anything like it, he waved her misgivings aside and continued his intense discussions with the signora. Indeed, when Lucy had admired the dress, much as she might a painting in a gallery, the owner had smiled but left her in no doubt that Signor Fortuny would decide.

And that was when the realisation hit her: he was dressing her. Dressing her in the best his money could buy, and clearly his money could buy the best. This, she thought, is not a present. This is not a small gift, or even a large one. And then she remembered the simple dress she had worn to the opera. Fortuny had said nothing about it at the time, but he had clearly thought much about it since. He thinks, she said to herself, watching with increasing amazement the discussion continuing in front of her, he thinks I'm not—what was the word?—polished enough, and she suddenly felt like a heroine from a Henry James novel. One of those young women who wandered into the oh-so-sophisticated land, the mysterious, even nefarious land of Old World assumptions that she, Lucy, naturally assumed were dead, to have been consigned to the dustbin of history for a hundred years.

Yet here she was, in the eyes of Fortuny and his accomplice, with her body exuding energy, vibrancy and freshness, being draped in the stylish accoutrements her New World freshness and energy lacked. It was quite a jolt. Does he—does she—still look at the world as if it were a nineteenth-century novel? A world whose centre was right here, and to which, from time to time, some returned from the outer margins to rejuvenate the centre with their energy? With the promise of new life? Oh, *they* might not see it like that, might not consciously think like that, but was that really what this was about?

And so she decided to tell Fortuny, once and for all, that there was really no need for gifts, that he'd already been too kind, that this *wasn't* how it was, that she didn't care about clothes. But just as she was about to say all of this, even to say that she found pursuing fashion as banal as pursuing the idea of love for all the wrong reasons, the signora emerged with a dress of the deepest, the most liquid red she'd ever seen, in the softest fabric she'd ever felt. And before she knew it, she was wearing it, running her palms over her hips, over this most extraordinarily textured material that seemed to have been cut to her every curve, and turning to face herself in the mirror.

Fortuny had risen from his chair, and seemed to be drifting towards her as if, having called some extraordinary creature into existence, he was now faced with the overwhelming question of what on earth to do with her, and what to do with himself. And the signora raised her palms to the heavens, acknowledging that the being for whom the garment had been intended had indeed come to earth. The twain had converged, and Lucy stood before them, as if having risen from the translucent waters of artistic creation to slip naturally into this exquisite red confection.

A few weeks later, Lucy met Fortuny at his house early one evening, from where they left, through the high and wide front door that opened onto the Grand Canal, to take a water taxi. It might have been easier, Fortuny remarked, to take the gondola across the canal and simply walk. They would, however, have then missed the view of the city that a trip along the canal offered. Lucy was puzzled at first: take the what? She remained silent on the damp steps of the doorway, wondering what on earth he meant. It was only when Fortuny repeated himself, in a dreamy, almost distant voice, a faraway look in his eyes, that she finally understood. He had pronounced gondola the Venetian way, the 'l' more or less a 'y', as in Spanish: gondo*y*a.

    She had already noticed that from time to time Fortuny would slip into Venetian pronunciation and the local, more guttural accent on a word here, a phrase there. This usually made for only small changes, but would alter whole words or change the sound of an entire sentence, completely throwing her—sometimes to the point where she could have sworn he was speaking another language altogether. And, of course, he was. At times like these she would hear her father's voice, hear McBride the amateur scholar, leaning back in that favourite armchair of his with John Julius Norwich's *Venice, The Rise To Empire* on his lap, and saying of the Venetians, 'They're not Italian, you know. They're different.' And Lucy would smile to herself in silent agreement and wonder what her father would make of her now, strolling to the front portal of Fortuny's house feeling as if she had been born to it.

Over the last few weeks she'd been to small functions, mostly gallery openings, with Fortuny. And, without anything actually being said, it seemed obvious that he was slowly introducing her into his society, gradually moulding her, with a suggestion here and there. Don't be too eager to please, he might say. Or, don't listen so intently when they talk to you, because they're not… And so on. These suggestions were never too much, never too insistent. They were delivered as friendly advice, in the manner of an insider explaining the rules of a rather amusing local game. A game that was, in the end, all a bit a lark that did no one any harm. And, taken in that spirit, Lucy didn't mind, but she was nonetheless aware that she was being tutored in the peculiarities and subtleties of foreign custom. She just didn't know the local rules—that was all Fortuny ever implied—and he, her guide, would teach her.

Did she know, he said one evening when she had slipped into quiet retreat as though suddenly finding the whole thing too much, did she know that when the model for Botticelli's *Birth of Venus* first arrived in Florence from the provinces—nobody knew where, she just appeared—she caused such a stir that everybody wanted to meet her, even just glimpse her. Everybody, and Botticelli too. This woman, who brought with her this indefinable elsewhere, was, Fortuny suggested, what we would now call a 'celebrity'.

'Was she Botticelli's mistress?' The question seemed natural, logical, but it occurred to Lucy as she asked it that she and Fortuny had never spoken of such things. Lucy had never been timid about sex. After the violinist who had disappeared to London, there had been other brief affairs, but she had always made sure she'd never got in over her head again, yet she now felt strangely self-conscious, as though she'd stepped over a tacitly understood boundary.

'Perhaps he was as in awe of this creature as everyone else,' Fortuny replied, shrugging as if to say, Who knows?

'The misery of people like us,' Lucy intoned with what she hoped was just the right theatricality, 'is that no one dares approach us.'

Fortuny suddenly turned to her, puzzled.

'Oh, not us, not you or me,' she added hastily. 'You must remember *The Duchess of Malfi*?'

But although Fortuny nodded, Lucy got the distinct impression that he didn't, or had simply never read Webster's play. Curious, she went on.

'It must be difficult, being unapproachable, when all you want to do is live.'

Fortuny stared at her, outwardly calm, inwardly thrown. What was she saying?

He'd pondered that question for days afterwards, long after he was convinced Lucy had forgotten all about it, but it had been a comment, he thought, that walked the fine line between innocence and experience, awareness and unawareness, the intentional and the utterly unintentional. And, for all his pondering, he could come to no conclusion about why she'd said it. Indeed, if it were an invitation, if it were her call, it was—he almost smiled to himself—a slippery one.

Now, as they walked to the front steps of his house, the question still vaguely lurking in some part of his mind, Fortuny casually turned to Lucy and was suddenly struck by the ease with which she stood in the vast frame of the doorway. He inwardly praised the brilliant, deep red of the dress she wore as he helped her onto the taxi, and silently congratulated himself on his taste and choice of garment. Most of the time he saw Lucy in the casual clothes of the young that she wore to her lessons—blue jeans, casual shirts, sloppy jumpers. But here, wearing the dress for the first time, and clasping his hand with an intriguing natural grace as she moved lightly over the mossy steps of the landing and onto the waiting craft, was a truly intoxicating creature. Classical.

The description occurred to Fortuny again and again throughout the evening. He noted the classical simplicity of everything she wore, from the lines of that dress to the single pin that just held her hair in check and the silver locket suspended from her neck. Here, quite clearly, was a young woman with an instinctive sense of grace just waiting to be drawn out, to be coaxed from her. And this night, it seemed that she had evolved, in a very short time, into the creature that she promised to become. And, once again, Fortuny was both lulled and alarmed by the song of this mermaid.

The craft tilted back slightly as they splashed into the canal, before passing the small square from which Lucy had first spied on Fortuny's balcony in the former life of her adolescence, and she gave it a backward glance before they passed under the wooden frame of the Accademia bridge. And all along the canal, with the waters gleaming orange and white beneath them, the dome of the Salute in front of them and the mauve haze of the Lido in the distance, Fortuny eyed her furtively. Lucy never took her eyes off the city, drinking in the sight of the massed old palaces of the waterway, gazing at the traditional landing point for diplomatic and official parties up ahead where the columns of San Marco and San Theodore stood in the twilight. Those Doges, she thought with a grin to herself, they knew a thing or two about arrivals and departures, about how to impress a visitor, for here the city was undeniably magisterial.

But they never reached the basin of San Marco or neared the landing that opened onto the square, for the craft slowed and turned into a smaller canal that led directly to the Fenice. Once again, Fortuny took her hand as they stepped off the boat near San Fantin and strolled through the first of the balmy summer nights towards the crowd.

The façade of the building was plain and simple enough. But inside, watching a new production of *Lucia di Lammermoor* from one of the five tiers of curved balconies, she thought again that it was like sitting in a vast, gilded music box. The performers on stage, the whole spectacle, emerged before her as if wound up by an invisible, governing hand that could, at any moment, reappear through the trompe l'oeil ceiling.

After the performance, Fortuny and Lucy moved through the crowded foyer, stopping here and there to chat with his friends and acquaintances. He introduced her as his young student, addressing her directly, in English, as 'my dear', and noting her growing ease on meeting these people. He also—more than pleased with himself—observed the stir she created, the heads that turned to follow her progress, recognising that elusive elsewhere that she brought with her. Fortuny's friends were curious now, asked questions of her, talked idly. And, almost as pleasing, nobody seemed surprised that he should be at the theatre with her. Or that she should be with him. As much as he had thought of himself as having grown old in the year since his retirement, society still saw him as it always had. Fortuny, who (all his friends agreed) must surely have made a pact with the devil, continued to defy the years to the extent that this creature could take her natural place beside him.

As the crowd thinned, most people wandered across the square to the small bars and the open pizzerias of San Marco. But others, Fortuny's acquaintances among them, made their way to the restaurant next door that specialised in late-night suppers for theatregoers. Lucy's deep red evening dress glowed in that group like a lantern, and when they stopped outside the restaurant, it seemed to Fortuny that everybody stood still for a moment while they gazed upon her, a slight hum in the air.

They left the group and, walking from the Campo San Fantin, Lucy, thirsty, stopped at a fountain and scooped water into her mouth. When she was finished, her body shivered and she shook the excess water from her lips and cheeks into the surrounding air. All the time, Fortuny stood by the fountain watching her, transfixed.

The Fenice, now deserted, but with its lights still shining, receded like an empty stage set as they took a taxi back to Fortuny's house. It was the first and last time Lucy ever attended a production there, for the next week the theatre burnt down, leaving only its façade to stand as a reminder of its celebrated past.

Lucy slowly sank into Fortuny's couch as if easing into a bubble bath while he poured her some wine into the same glass she had admired after their visit to *Madama Butterfly*. Fortuny, it seemed to her on nights such as these, was not the maestro, and she was not the student. Such divisions were cast aside like a school uniform being thrown away for the summer. During their outings he had only placed his arm about her once or twice to guide her across a crowded lane. He did this with consideration and a lightness of touch that she knew quite well came with an almost palpable restraint, making their brief moments of physical contact—like the way his fingers guided hers across the strings during their lessons—all the more significant.

One evening the previous week, Lucy had arrived early and had been let in by Rosa, who had pointed her up to the *portego* then disappeared. Lucy had walked to the balcony but there had been no sign of Fortuny and she'd stepped back into the hall. From there, through a half-opened door, she'd been able to see into one of the rooms that ran off the *portego*—a room officially referred to as the Red Room because of the patterned cloth, designed and made by Fortuny himself, on its walls. A modern lamp, the room's one concession to progress, threw out a clear light and she

could see a silver chandelier and a large painting of a
Venetian street scene in the style of Carpaccio. Surely
it couldn't be a Carpaccio... But why not? She also
caught a glimpse of two small black and white portraits, one of a bald-headed man in uniform, the other
a pencil sketch of an old woman. There was music is-
suing from behind the door and the recording was so
familiar she could almost see the notes. It was a work
of Fortuny's, a recording she had often practised to.

She was listening to the music and gazing at the portraits when suddenly, reflected in a gold-framed mirror that hung above an ornate mantelpiece next to the
pictures, she witnessed the spectacle of Fortuny listening to Fortuny.

She had heard that W. H. Auden spent his last years
reading nothing but the poetry of W. H. Auden and had
always thought of that as an intolerable conceit. But now,
here was Fortuny, lost in his own world. As she watched
in the mirror, she could see his hands moving in mid-air,
attempting to emulate the intricate movements, the slurs,
the *fermatae*, the runs, that years ago would have been
second nature to him. And she knew that he would be
physically incapable of such playing now.

Lucy had slipped back out onto the balcony and sat
watching the lights on the water, vowing never to arrive early again. When Fortuny at last emerged from
the room, he apologised for keeping her, said he'd been
reading, had lost all track of time...

Now, strains of this evening's opera still in her ears, Lucy rose in search of a breeze and stood by the open window, the red of her dress glowing in the evening light. Fortuny had eschewed the wine and carefully sipped his favourite Calvados. A faint scent of spring jasmine and lilacs wafted in from the courtyard and lingered in the room. Framed by the window, Lucy looked down into the yard like a pensive figure in some domestic scene depicted by a Flemish painter.

And it was then, as she stared down into the garden, recalling Fortuny's face as she'd first seen it on a record sleeve—the strong, confident eyes that gave no hint of the man who now relived his former glories behind closed doors—that Fortuny requested she stay standing exactly where she was. Lucy turned.

'Your head,' he murmured, with a slight wave of his hand like a film director. 'A little higher.'

'Like this?' she asked, indulging him but making sure with the smile in her eyes and an ironic note in her voice that he knew he was being indulged. His gaze was fixed—concentrated but removed—lapsing into some private reminiscence, unaware of her as other than a figure at the window.

Lucy sensed then that she wasn't the first to stand there, perhaps not the first to take the pose he had requested. She almost spoke, almost asked, What is it? What do you see? But, instead, she simply stared into Fortuny's eyes, as if into a peephole. And, not for the first time, she became aware of the ghosts of the house, the voices, the guests, the parties; wondered what it must have been like to know Fortuny then. She imagined the discreet evenings when a woman might have stood by the same window, posing much as she herself was now. Possibly a passing affair, possibly not important in itself. A vaguely remembered figure, important only for the promise held in her presence.

Somehow, Lucy was convinced as she watched the still, seated figure of Fortuny that she had prompted the memory of an incidental moment, the open window a view onto the past. She watched Fortuny, saw him close his eyes, seemingly drifting off.

Lucy thought of her father in the years just after her mother's death, sitting in his large padded armchair, closing his eyes and leaning his head back in much the same way as Fortuny did now. But she always knew McBride was never at rest. He would be frowning, always frowning, his body and hands tense. At those moments she would blow gently into his ear then tap his nose, and the lines of the frown would dissolve into laughter. Sometimes. It was a game, one that gave her pleasure, and a childlike sense of power to think that only she could bring the laughter back to his eyes.

Impulsively, she moved from the window and sat down gently beside Fortuny, pursed her lips and blew into his ear, creating a faint whistle. His eyes opened instantly. He smiled and, with an almost childlike wonder in his eyes, reached out his hand to Lucy, his fingers now touching her cheeks, softly, slowly falling across her cheek to her chin, as if reassuring himself of her actuality, her living warmth.

'Why have you never fallen in love?'

It was the first personal question he had asked her. She grinned. 'A kind, sullen star I was lucky to be born under.' Then she laughed. 'Besides, I'm too busy to fall in love.'

Fortuny laughed too and the trance passed. When she finally rose, he thanked her for the evening, almost bowing, then thanked her again, his palms touching, his fingers clasped in front of him. Lucy picked up her bag. There was really no need for *him* to thank *her*.

The lamps were lit in the salon and, as Lucy shut the door leading to the courtyard, she noticed Fortuny walking towards Venus, the young woman who'd caused such a stir in the streets of Florence four hundred years ago. He moved as if the room were crowded after all, and he were about to engage in conversation with an old friend.

That very morning, in fact, Carla had visited Fortuny. She was sad because she had not heard from him in such a long time. Had she offended her old friend in some way and, if so, how? He shook his head and reassured her that this was not at all the case.

Carla had leaned forward, puzzled.

'Is it the girl?'

Fortuny narrowed his gaze. 'What do you mean?'

Carla paused, then nodded to herself. She had her confirmation.

'Paolo,' she said confidentially, leaning forward far enough in her seat to lightly touch his sleeve with fingers that dripped with the last of her gold rings, 'I know the power of a young woman. I once had it. But, Paolo, don't forget old friends, eh?'

Now, settled in the armchair in his study, he thought about Lucy. He recalled the image of her standing in front of the window and, again hearing Carla's words from that morning, dissolved into a world of speculation. In front of him, spread out on the walnut table, was the parchment depicting the family tree. As always, his finger came to rest on the last entry, Paolo Fortuny. And he whispered the name to the still evening air, to the room, resisting this time the usual epithet, for the mood was not upon him.

Chapter Nine

OUTSIDE, Lucy could smell rain. Somewhere over the lagoon she heard faint thunder and reached into her bag for her scarf, to find she must have left it behind at Fortuny's. She ducked past the hotel at the end of the lane, its lights on, its doors as open as the watchful eyes of the old lady at the desk, the concierge who missed nothing. She walked past the familiar black and white cat sitting on the front mat. It was always the same, and Lucy guessed what the old woman was thinking behind the shutters of her eyes. But in all her comings and goings they never acknowledged each other and, in time, their silence had become almost conspiratorial.

Sensing rain, Lucy was hurrying up the dimly lit calle when she almost crashed into a dark figure. The hotel cat, alert to movement, was staring impassively from the mat, the old lady had leaned forward on her desk, and Lucy looked up from the stones of the small street to meet a pair of deep green eyes and pale, painted cheeks. The figure, wrapped in a black cloak, stared back from under a three-cornered hat. She almost gasped her apologies, when she realised it was a Carnivale dummy.

She stepped back, eye to eye with the object but still not quite convinced it wasn't about to leap into life any moment. What was it doing there? The mask shop was closed, its lights off, but somehow the owner had left the dummy in the street. Now it would be rained on, its paint would run and its proud feathers would be drenched and matted by morning.

At the top of the calle she glanced back at the dummy before turning up towards San Salvatore and home. She half expected it to be gone, but it wasn't and the solitariness of it plagued her. *Why have you never fallen in love?* Of course, Fortuny knew the answer to his question. He had known it all along. He'd just returned from the many crowded rooms of his youth to the empty salons of his present when he'd asked her, and it was only now, hurrying home before the rain, that Lucy heard the caution in his voice. Don't, it said, be so casual with love, or one day love will be casual with you.

Lucy sauntered through those leaning and winding lanes that would eventually lead her through to the open space of the Campo Santa Margherita where she was bound to find familiar faces. In the long, open square she could hear the sound of pop music from the cafés, the shrieks, the excited calls of friends and strangers, tourists and locals, and smell the perfume and smoke from the crowd. Among the throng, there were her friends from the Conservatorium.

It was only when she sat down to join them and saw their expressions as they gaped at her dress, its quality and cut of fabric that no student could ever afford, that she remembered what she was wearing, And as she studied their eyes and read the conclusions a few were drawing behind them, she wished she'd never succumbed to the impulse to seek them out. Someone, possibly to break the silence, remarked that they had seen her out with Fortuny, and smiled at her as though an explanation were required and the whole business a matter of public interest. Lucy knew that she was now acquainted with the kind of Venetian society that her student friends had never met and only ever heard about. She refused to be drawn but they went on, prodding her.

'He's old,' Lucy finally blurted out, wishing she'd never said it. It was not only insulting to Fortuny but she could see that nobody believed her—Fortuny's reputation for triumphing over time was widespread. 'He wants a companion,' she went on. 'Someone for social occasions. He's used to having somebody with him so he asked me. That's all.'

The light, teasing talk stopped immediately and the table fell silent. Everybody looked down, allowing the moment to pass, and when conversation started again it was quiet, confined to pockets about the table. She was in the way. They would, no doubt, speak more freely about her when she was gone.

When she rose (everybody's eyes again drawn irresistibly to her dress), Marco, who had said nothing until now, rose with her. Since he had met her that first day at the station they had become friends, closer than any of the other friendships she'd made at the school. A native of Venice, named after its patron saint, he was in love with his city and, she knew, in love with her.

His adoration was of the quiet kind. He quietly waited for her when rehearsals or classes finished, hung about watching her when small social groups like this evening were breaking up. All for a chance to be alone with her, speak to her, to convey, through the delicacy or concern of his gestures, the nature of his feelings. He leapt at the occasional chance to take Lucy's arm and guide her across a narrow, crowded bridge, to point out short cuts, houses of interest and secret places as he ushered her through the network of streets, alleys and squares of his city. But it was mostly in his eyes that Lucy saw the longing of someone who could look upon, but never possess, the object of his longing. She saw all of this, but could find only gratitude for his kindness.

As they walked the final stretch to Lucy's flat, Marco spoke of Fortuny.

'You should be watchful.'

His tone annoyed her. 'He's lonely. I keep him company sometimes,' she insisted.

'Not so lonely.'

'What do you mean?'

'I mean,' Marco said, 'he has some powerful friends.'
He paused. 'In the region. Friends you would not see.
Not nice people.'

'You mean political friends?'

Marco nodded, frowning.

'Oh, Marco, Marco. I don't know anything about
politics and I don't care about it. Nor does he. He's just
afraid of being alone.'

But Marco shook his head, speaking, as he always
did to Lucy, in English.

'I know these people. Their type.'

She laughed. 'Their *type*?'

Marco ignored her laughter.

'They're still—' and here he waved his hand regally
in the air '—living the days of *La Serenissima*. They
wouldn't give you the time of day if they thought you
were just a tourist. They would give you nothing.'

'What do you mean?' Lucy was growing angry.

'Nothing is free. This city runs, has always run, on
money. *Schee.* On something for something. There is
always a price.'

He looked pointedly at her outrageously expensive
dress, and Lucy suddenly saw herself through the eyes
of Marco and the others. Kept. The word froze si-

lently in her mind. Paid for. A tart living it up on the old man's money. Their crude assumptions were so unjust, so unfounded, but they knew nothing of the truth. How could they? How could they know the power of the dream that had brought her here? They could not possibly know, she told herself again and again, as shame mingled with indignation.

Then her voice was rising and somewhere tears were not far away. 'I trained to his music, listened to it, absorbed it, lived it,' she said in a rush, then breathed in deeply to calm herself. 'It helped me through a very difficult time when I was younger, a girl. For years, before I ever met him, Fortuny gave me great pleasure through his playing. And now,' she said, stopping at her door and gazing into the still, green canal in front of her, 'I have the opportunity to give some of that pleasure back.'

Marco was listening without looking at her. Lucy leaned back against her door and said quietly, 'There's no need to be watchful. It's a large house and I'm sure it feels very empty. He just needs a companion sometimes.'

Marco lingered about the door as she turned the key in the lock. She knew that he would never ask to come in, would always wait to be invited, but Lucy suggested they meet another time. She was tired, she said, but in truth she was annoyed with what was, after all, a small, regional city, with its rumours and its gossip. A town.

* * *

Just after four o'clock in the morning, Lucy was sitting at her bedroom table writing to her father, describing the events of the last few weeks and making more mention of the kindness of Signor Fortuny. She was a light sleeper, often troubled by sounds in the night, by dreams. Especially by dreams. She could be woken by the slap of a flyscreen door, like a slap to the face, and see once again the ungrateful daughter storming from the house while Molly sits at the kitchen table, head buried deep in her hands, waiting for the heatwave and the headaches to pass. Or she could hear the thin strains of the saddest of music, echoing about a dark and empty home, an offering to Molly that would always be too late, dispatched without hope, into the dark temperate infinity.

She'd put the red dress away when she got in. How could they possibly know of something that had started all those years ago? And she would see it through. Something (the saddest of music, the sweetest of aches, the most enchanting of myths—mysterious to her even now) had entered her all those years before, and would not leave her until the thing was seen through right to the end. How could they know, and how could she tell them? There was only one person on earth to whom she could bring this thing and be sure that she would be taken in and understood. And she also sensed that, as soon as she offered it up for explanation and it became understood so that she could look upon it and say, 'Yes, that's it, I see it now. That's what it was,' she would take the mystery from it. And by making it explicable, and gaining the distance to understand it all herself, she would have lost it. And she would see that it was always going to be lost anyway. But first it had to be lived, to be seen through. That was the price of dreams. For Marco was right—these things did have a price, but not the price he imagined.

Their lessons continued, but at these times Fortuny was a different person, more distant, not the man who escorted her to the opera, the theatre and other social functions. He was Fortuny the Maestro. The impersonal Fortuny. Lofty, even. That figure on a mountaintop, surveying all below it. Of course, he never said as much, but his manner suggested it. This, he was saying, was the nature of the artist. Physically moving through society's streets, houses and public buildings, but all the time remaining untouched by them. Smiling, nodding, living, but always with that detached core that remained oblivious to all else, complete in itself. He was the artist, as unmoved by the world as a catalyst was by the chemical change it facilitated. Let the crazy, madcap world do whatever it will to itself, the artist remained undisturbed.

This, it seemed to Lucy, was the nature of the Fortuny who sat quietly and listened throughout her lessons. It was all part of this thing that had brought her here, this sweetest of aches, this most enchanting of myths. And it was at times such as these, when his talk would fall into a kind of regal idiom: 'one' simply knows such and such, and so on. At first, the sheer sweep of his statements and the sense of authority that accompanied them had made him seem beyond questioning. But, lately, Lucy had found something irritating, almost fragile, and even absurd about the whole pose, the attitude he struck when speaking, the lofty tone of his voice.

One day, sitting at the piano, she casually remarked on a performer she'd been listening to recently. Fortuny would possibly have known him, she suggested, a contemporary of his, but one that she had only just discovered. He was not well known, but she thought him well worth hearing. Fortuny was mildly curious and listened to what she had to say, his elbows resting on the arms of the small chair he used for their lessons, both hands under his chin, his fingertips lightly touching. Serene. Detached.

But the moment Lucy mentioned the musician's name, Fortuny was transformed. The studied pose dissolved, his hands dropped to his lap, and he spoke in a tone of obvious annoyance, which attempted to pass itself off as dismissive boredom.

'He was a fool.'

'Why?'

'Why?' His voice echoed about the walls of the salon, his clean, square jaw pushed forward. 'You have to ask why?'

Lucy was quiet for a moment, allowing some calm to return to Fortuny's manner before speaking again.

'I only said that his style was interesting.'

'The man never possessed an artistic nature. Never knew a creative moment, never felt his heart skip a beat until he finally fell over and died on a supermarket floor in California.' Then, staring at the window, he said, 'May he live on in muzak.'

At first, Lucy was too stunned to reply.

'Never listen to the mediocre,' he said, breaking the silence.

'Fortuny—'

'Do you understand?' he said, almost calm again.

'But, Fortuny—'

He cut her off. 'You must understand this.'

'Yes. But what do you mean by the "mediocre"?'

'It doesn't need to be explained. One simply knows, or one doesn't.'

'Does one?'

'The real thing, my dear Lucy. The real thing.' He spoke now as if addressing a bright child. 'If you can't pick it, you can't create it. Never listen to the mediocre!'

He then swung round to face the window, as if

nothing more needed to be said. It was, she realised, another test. But of what? Loyalty? It was absurd. He was bullying her again, and she wouldn't be bullied.

'Fortuny,' she said again, calmly and deliberately, as his head slowly turned towards her. 'I will listen to anybody I choose to. I will not be told. You do not have the right. I will not be told what I can and cannot do.'

He watched her for a moment as if weighing the matter up, then he rose sharply from his chair, walked to the piano and slammed it shut. Lucy jumped back as he spoke.

'Then you are a fool, too. A little fool with a scatterbrain, and I have no time for scatterbrained little fools,'

It was sudden and—she was shocked by the thought—it was almost violent. Could those hands, those arms, that had created the saddest of music, also inflict physical pain? She felt a passing moment of alarm but he walked away, the discordant sound of the piano still reverberating through the salon, and added a final pronouncement on his way to the *portego*. 'The lesson is over.'

Lucy, still stunned, watched him go but, as he reached the doorway, he paused, looked back at her and said, 'There is no need for you to return. Our lessons are concluded.'

'Good!'

Madam always had the last word, and she wasn't changing her habits now.

Then he was gone. Lucy sat there a moment, then shook her head and slowly stooped to pick up her carry bag. She stood up and walked towards the courtyard, slamming the large, old door behind her.

In his study that night Fortuny was preoccupied with what had happened, with Lucy's casual mention of this Blum. Blum, the young cellist who had died on a supermarket floor in California and was doomed to live on in muzak. Or was he? Odd, he hadn't thought of him for years, not since they'd been students. And why should he have? They'd never been friends as much as friendly rivals. But they had studied together in Rome and people had inevitably compared them because they had been the best of their year.

Then Blum had gone to America and made muzak. At least, Fortuny thought it was muzak. But lately there had been a series of articles written about him, some of them quite glowing. He had been an artist ahead of his time, they said, a Satie of the cello whose time had finally come. Of course, it was all rubbish, and Fortuny had thrown the articles away without even bothering to finish them. An artist should always die young, he had once said to Carla with deep sarcasm. But, privately, he asked himself, where were the retrospectives on Fortuny? Nowhere. Nobody, since his retirement, had taken him up, and outside Venice he was convinced he had sunk like a stone.

But later, as he sipped his Calvados, his anger subsided, and the next morning, one of brilliant sunshine,
he regretted having lost his temper with Lucy. That afternoon he sent her a card of apology with a small selection of courtyard flowers, delivered by Rosa.

Lucy smiled to herself as she closed the door on
Rosa, whose disapproving stare clearly said, This young
woman is trouble. She placed the flowers in a vase and
meditatively turned them in the sun before leaving to
join Marco and another student friend, who played the
double bass, in the square.

Lucy barely recognised the tinkle of the piano as her
own, and succumbed to the pleasure of simply playing for fun on these evenings far more easily than she
had thought she would. And Marco, standing by the
piano, fiddle in hand, seemed to have forgotten all
about the 'words' they'd had when they'd last met. He
grinned all through a Noël Coward number, and even
though (unusually for a Venetian) he didn't smoke, he
wedged a cigarette holder à la Coward between his
teeth. When the number finished he turned to Lucy,
blowing imaginary smoke into the air, and said, 'I'm
just *med* about you.' He gazed round at the lights of
the square. 'God, I love English. They're always *med*
about each other.'

One song blended into another, and as the hours
drained from the evening, Lucy remembered, with a

bit of a jolt, that at some stage of the afternoon when she'd found herself thinking about playing this evening, looking forward to it even, the thought *I'll see Marco tonight* had passed across her mind, lifted her, puzzled her, then been forgotten. Until now.

He was the one they all said was going places, and, watching him, listening to him play even the simplest tunes, Lucy could tell that every note had a touch of that something extra about it. She nodded to herself, acknowledging that they all just might be right, that Marco might indeed be going places, may even, indeed—and she half smiled—be the real thing.

A few days later Fortuny was giving voice to an internal debate, an addendum to Blum. True artists, one had to understand, were a rarity, and so too were the true appreciators and interpreters of their art. He was, he said, reminded of a famous scientist who had once said to him that, after years of study and research, there were only a handful of people in the world capable of appreciating what he was doing.

'It's the same—' and here he gestured towards Lucy sitting at the cello '—with our art. You have to be prepared to be lonely. Do you understand?'

'Yes.' She nodded. She knew exactly what he meant, more than he realised.

'And maybe all for nothing. What do the Americans call it?' He hummed to himself for a moment, trying to remember the elusive phrase. Then he looked at her, disconsolate. 'A mug's game.'

It was the first time Fortuny had made even an oblique reference to having achieved less in his art than he had hoped for or anticipated. The uncertainty, for the first time, was clearly evident. By lonely, among other things, he meant unnoticed. And the point of those at the Conservatorium who had dismissively described him as a large fish in a small lagoon was brought home to her for the first time.

Standing in the courtyard, she thought about those sacred notions of Fortuny's art, which transcended the everyday and the ordinary in the same way that his family history did. It all seemed suddenly to be out of her reach, as if membership to the sacred society of the elect was predetermined and no amount of study and work could change what was, what had already been written. Without consciously acknowledging as much, she'd always dreamed that the world of the elect—of true artists—might one day be hers too. She had felt that she was only waiting to enter it and that her collaboration with Fortuny was a collaboration of equals, yet something in his manner had unnerved her. What if she weren't so special after all?

But she had almost come to the point where she felt she was living a story, and was too deep into the tale to turn back even if she wanted to. The tale had taken over, and she had no choice but to go with it. A young

girl is roused from her sleep by the saddest of music.
She rises from her garden chair, she follows the music,
follows her thread, and it leads her here, into this
courtyard of mellowed morning light, where it always
was going to lead.

PART FOUR

Chapter Ten

A WAVE of hot midsummer nights rolled over the city, enfolded it. The windows in the salon were thrown open. Holding an emptied glass of grappa, Lucy turned to Fortuny from the couch; his sleeves were rolled up and, once again, she noted the strength of his forearms, his robustness. She was smiling the smile of someone holding on to a secret, but at the point of finally offering it up. Fortuny, seated in his armchair in front of her, stared back at her, pleasantly puzzled.

'What is it?' he said.

Lucy grinned, closed her eyes, opened them again, studied Fortuny a moment, then let the thing slip from her.

'You won't remember, but I wrote to you once,' she said.

Fortuny was no longer puzzled but confused.

'Wrote to me? When?'

'Years ago.' Lucy laughed. 'I was still at school.'

Still dwelling on the memory, she poured herself another drink, then laughed again, staring at the floor, slowly shaking her head.

'I had your records. Your photo.'

She looked up. Fortuny was completely still now.

'My photo?'

'It was on your record cover.'

'And you kept it?' Fortuny's face was now relaxing into a smile.

'Yes.'

'How old were you?'

'Thirteen, fourteen. I can't remember.'

She lied. She knew the year, she knew the day.

'And you wrote?'

'Yes. A little later.'

'That was very daring.'

'It was.'

Fortuny was now jovial.

'Did I reply?'

'Yes.' She laughed.

'Just as well.' Fortuny smiled.

'I never thanked you.'

'The pleasure was mine.'

Lucy then described the photograph and Fortuny laughed again.

'Oh, that.' He chuckled. 'It was taken in Rome. I've forgotten when now.'

'1962.' Lucy grinned.

'It was a nightmare. Everybody was on each other's

nerves,' he said, waving his hand. 'But why did you write?'

Lucy grinned again, but inwardly. 'I was copying one of your pieces.'

'Which one?'

'I don't know now. But you did something during it and I didn't know what, so I asked you.'

'And I didn't tell you.' Fortuny smiled.

'No.'

'You had a cheek, asking,' he said, clearly amused.

They were both quiet for a while. A slight breeze came through the opened windows of the low-lit salon. Lucy leaned back on the couch, her voice now soft in confession.

'I kept that letter.'

Fortuny was silent for a moment, then got up from his chair. 'The misery of people like us,' he murmured to himself, 'is that no one dares approach us.' What had she meant? Had it been an invitation or a challenge?

Lucy watched him as he stooped over the small serving table. His silvery hair was in need of cutting and for a moment she imagined brushing it back with her fingers, telling him that he should be more mindful of it. In the same moment she also caught a glimpse of Fortuny the Younger, the confident cellist, the celebrity. Fortuny, the lover. For she knew that he had had many love affairs over the years, and had continued to live in the manner of a young man throughout his life. And, as she stared at him, she was slowly realising that even though it was the photograph of the young Fortuny she'd fallen in love with, it was the Fortuny standing before her, the *lived* Fortuny, the Fortuny whose face bore the marks of experience, that now drew her in. She was dwelling on this, and why it should be, when he suddenly looked up and caught the curiosity in her stare.

He smiled, and then, as if she had somehow summoned him, he came and sat beside her on the couch. For a long time he said nothing, only took the tiniest sips from his glass and gazed at the darkness of the windows. Lucy watched him. He was perfectly still, could almost have been meditating, emptying his mind of the useless thoughts that cluttered a day, and contemplating what she'd just told him. Content with the silence, she too stared ahead—at the walls, the paintings, the decorated glass—and became so absorbed in the portrait of a young woman dressed in the style of the 1940s that she almost forgot Fortuny's presence.

It was then, in his low, almost guttural voice, that he spoke. And not even directly to her, but to the air. And not in Italian, or English, or any language she'd ever heard. If, indeed, it was a language. All she heard was this sound, low, guttural, soft. A chant, almost. Or a song. And as he continued, she began to feel its rhythms, to discern sentences, and became enthralled, slowly transported by a sound, by a language so elemental it didn't require comprehension or meaning, it was simply *felt*. A sound that seemed to emerge from some dark corner of history where it had lain in wait for its moment to rise, for its destined listener, for the right ear into which it might pour its loneliness, for the very person who would understand without need of comprehension, to simply feel the sound without need of articulation. The effect was hypnotic. Fortuny continued, his voice still low, but rich, like no voice she'd ever heard, like the saddest of music. And she was about to ask what this language was, and what it all meant, when she found herself watching the slow descent of his hand through the air. Slowly, it fell. Mesmerising. Falling through the air, through the years. And she knew then it had always been falling. She watched his hand, almost nodding, recognising, knowing the moment. A gesture so natural, so fluid, light, that she barely felt his fingers as they landed on the skin of her knee where her dress had parted. Intrigued, she watched as his hand slowly stroked her knee, circling the skin, then slowly trailing along her leg.

He made no clumsy attempts to kiss or embrace her, neither did he speak to her or look for a reaction from her. He, too, was watching the movement of his own fingers. A moment so complete, so whole, that it seemed to leave them both spectators. A moment almost independent of them. Together, they watched it happen.

She glanced at his face, now young, his silver hair, now dark in the half-light, falling over his brow. Then she looked straight ahead to the portrait of the woman dressed in the style of the 1940s that she had been idly contemplating only a few moments before. In some distant part of her mind she was vaguely wondering what her name might have been, her background, and where she had posed, for the painting's setting seemed to be Fortuny's salon. She was speculating on what her mannerisms might have been, her language, the sound of her voice. Where she was now and if she were still alive, wondered whether she was a regular visitor to Fortuny's salon or if she had once been his lover…

Far away, she noted the parting of her legs and felt the distant touch of Fortuny's fingers, the expert fingers of Fortuny the Lover, his caresses producing a deep ache, intense yet sweet. Wistful. She sank further into the couch, as if sinking into another age altogether, retrieving and experiencing all its physical sensations. Then a climax, surprising even to Lucy in its suddenness. She closed her eyes, all thoughts of the woman in the painting gone. Behind her eyes, Fortuny appeared to her with a brooding, studio stare, part of his face artfully cast in shadow. She could smell the musty, damp scent of the music store that day as it mingled with the scents, now, in this room, a delirious tang in the air. A weight as heavy as any first love finally falling, falling from her, its sweet release, dazzling and light; sheet music and those long, desperate days of youth.

He watched her as she relaxed. Lucy lay back on the couch, cushions tumbling to the floor, her legs still parted, her eyes still closed. Her hair had remained perfectly combed and pinned throughout, the blouse she wore still neatly buttoned and ironed. It was only as the eye passed down her body that the scene unravelled, Fortuny thought, casually, almost playfully arresting the viewer's eyes, the half of her body that remained clothed accentuating the sudden glimpse of the unbuttoned skirt, the parted legs. The deep tan that had once been a feature of her legs was gone, but it was clearly the type of skin that would easily regain its tropical glow. All perfectly still, a young woman sleeping, the healthy sleep of a young Venus after play.

Behind her closed eyes, she could feel his gaze. She was both there in the room and not there, suspended between two worlds, the world that once was, and the world that the years had now led her to.

At last she opened her eyes, and there was Fortuny, now silent, his song done. Fortuny, the most gentle, the most considerate of lovers. The *lived* Fortuny, with the years in his eyes. And it was then that she rose, it seemed to him, like a dreamer from sleep, or like the spirit that inhabited a canvas suddenly rousing herself and rising from the translucent waters lapping about her feet.

He watched Lucy's dark eyes, steady as they rose to meet him. He felt her lips lightly on his cheek, and, simultaneously, the tug of her fingers as she undid his belt and loosened his trousers. He started. What was she doing?

'Please, my dear.'

Yes, yes, his eyes implored, they would have their moment, but not here. In Fortuny's plan they would now retire to his bedroom, where Rosa would have left chocolates and wafers and wine. But Lucy continued.

'No, my dear. Please.'

He was about to protest again, raise his voice, let her know what she clearly couldn't know, the wonderful surprise he had in store, that his bed awaited them, and wine, and wafers…when he felt the first sudden spasm of pleasure begin to stir his body from the cool depths of a long sleep.

Pleasure. Fortuny no longer even tasted the tang of an orange, was no longer uplifted by champagne or soothed by wine. It was as though the ordinary pleasures of life were unavailable to him now. Would always be lost and unavailable, never to be tasted again, never regained since the music stopped and the cello was put away; gone since that night a year before when the young singer, Sophia, had slipped from his room, leaving the wine untouched, the chocolates uneaten. But here, once again, was pleasure, and he sat, unmoving now, as the blood in his veins rushed to meet and respond to her young fingers.

Soon he closed his own eyes, responding to her, to the pleasure of the moment. But he sensed that she was moving, felt her hand leave him briefly, and when he opened his eyes she was standing before him with her skirt raised above her thighs. Quickly. Smoothly. Living the inevitable outcome of a dull day in a colonial city music store, releasing the thing that had brought her across the seas, across the years, to be here—the still secret she had kept throughout the eternity of adolescence—she lowered herself onto him, Fortuny, once more a lover.

With his tie still neat and the dress handkerchief still in his breast pocket, Fortuny leaned back on a pile of cushions. Lucy moved upon him, slowly, gently, so as not to disturb the stillness of the moment. Then, suddenly, his heart went deathly still, arrested by a terrifying wave of the deepest green.

Fortuny's eyes remained closed afterwards, a silent tribute to the young woman who had brought such magic with her, grateful that she had brushed aside his protests. This, and here he opened his eyes, this healthy young Venus had bestowed her gift upon him.

They were both slumped on the couch, still and silent. No need for words. Judging his moment, Fortuny adjusted his summer trousers, raised his finger, signalling he had something for her, then disappeared. He returned with a tray of chocolates, wafers and a bottle of grappa, which they set upon with the relish, it seemed to him, of young lovers.

'What,' she suddenly asked, crunching the lightest of wafers, 'what *was* that language?'

He smiled, resting his grappa on the couch upon which they both sat, Lucy at ease in half-nakedness.

'Venetian. Dialect.'

She stopped crunching. 'It was beautiful.'

Fortuny nodded. 'It is.'

'What does it say?'

'It is an old song. So old, nobody knows how old or where it is from. It says I have travelled across oceans, over fields, over the years, to be here.'

Of course. Of *course* it would say that. And, of course, it would be Fortuny who would give it voice. How could she tell the others? The only one she could tell about this thing that had crossed seas and fields and years to be here was Fortuny himself. And he knew, of course, without being told.

Later, he watched Lucy slip back into her garments, then rise, effortlessly, from the couch to gather her things. She paused by him as she passed, then bent over, wetted the tips of her fingers, touched his forehead and slowly closed his eyes. Then, like a dream-weaver moving through the unconscious, her work done, the dream lived, she slowly walked towards the door.

Fortuny took leave of her in the warm night air, silently. Neither of them spoke. Her fingers trailed along the railings of the steps. He watched those long, slender fingers, their touch still upon him. They'd sought him out like the fingers of the blind, pausing here and there, reviving dead nerves, stirring old blood, bringing back to life a whole order of feeling and sensation that had lain low in the comfortable routines of retired life. Lucy disappeared into the courtyard, stooped beneath the hanging branches of wisteria, and was gone, her fingers now plunged into her pockets, her strides bouncing with youth. And, knowing that she was watched, she never looked back.

They were surely the two halves of a single, converging destiny, and the promise of this young woman stayed with Fortuny like the lingering sensation of her touch. As the courtyard door shut and she left his frame of vision, he even felt settle upon him the tantalising notion that nothing less than the imperatives of a long family history had called up this fabulous creature.

He closed the door, turned to the *portego* and, like a young man after an all-night party, walked towards what he knew would be the deepest of sleeps.

Lucy had no memory of making her way home. She entered her flat like a sleepwalker, holding fast to a dream, determined to stave off the waking moment so that everything might continue as it was, and she would not suddenly stir and find herself in an unfamiliar town.

She lay down in a room still warm from the day's sun, the shadows of Fortuny's touch still prickling her skin, and sank into the drugged sleep of an overnight traveller, closing her eyes to everything about her, re-inhabiting the many rooms of Fortuny's salon, remembering the fall of his hand and the dull flop of cushions tumbling endlessly from the couch to the salon floor.

Lucy woke to moonlight, a moon so strong it may well have been a streetlight. Or a lamp. She'd forgotten to close the curtains and the room was frosted white, but it was stuffy and she threw open the window and leaned out into the cool night air. The rush of a faint breeze, the smell of the canal below and the touch of the crumbling wall rendering beneath her fingers told her she was no longer the dreamer, that the moment of waking had arrived and she had stirred to a dark town after all. The events of the evening returned, but, curiously, she was already detached from them. She was no longer the Lucy who had heard the distant tumble of cushions, but the Lucy who now ran her palms over the rough windowsill and whose lips were dry with the faint aftertaste of grappa.

That morning she sat in Marco's flat, a melancholy silence hanging over her. They were compiling a playing list of music for their work in the square. She toyed with a teaspoon, stared into her cup and occasionally tapped the saucer. She looked up as Marco entered the room with bundles of manuscripts in his arms. His kitchen table was covered with sheets of light music scored for violin, piano and accordion. Popular tunes, film themes and clichés from Ravel and Vivaldi.

It was a hot day and the reds and pinks of the geranium pot-plants that lined the ledge of the open window glared back at the sun. The room was bright and so were the objects in it—a bold red cup, yellow flowers, the colourful jackets of books. Marco's violin was visible on its stand by the wall in the adjoining room.

'Here,' Marco said, speaking in English as usual and smiling as he dropped the bundle onto the table. 'We can choose from any of them.'

He was smiling, pleased with himself, and clearly enjoying the excursion into a little light music. But Lucy was staring at the flowers and hearing the echo of the strangest words, a song sung in an incomprehensible language coming back at her as if from somebody else's dream, carrying with it the memory of things that had happened to somebody else—somebody else's memories, retrieved through somebody else's dreams. She turned to Marco.

'You choose.'

He frowned, puzzled. 'You don't want to?' he asked.

'I trust you.'

He shrugged his shoulders, hesitated for a moment,

then placed the sheets of music on his lap, calling out the titles before dropping them into two piles beside him on the floor.

But towards the bottom of the pile, with still no response to anything from Lucy, he suddenly stopped.

'You're not listening.'

She paused before replying, as if having only distantly heard.

'I'm not?'

He shook his head and dropped the rest of the sheets onto the floor, watching them spill across the polished marble.

'We'll do this another time.'

'I'm sorry.'

'You suggested this. You said you wanted to.'

'I know.'

'But you didn't.'

Lucy shook her head, while Marco rested his elbows on the table, staring at her as if trying to piece together a puzzle.

'Why did you call, then?'

'I don't know.'

'You can visit any time,' he quietly insisted.

'Thank you.'

'You don't need a reason.'

'No.'

Marco took her hand gently and Lucy closed her eyes, allowing herself the warmth and comfort of registering a slight squeeze as he repeated himself. 'You don't.'

It was the nearest Marco had ever come to saying anything. She slipped her hand free, registering his slender, violinist's fingers that everyone said were going places, his hands, still resting in the centre of the table, closing back in on themselves like a shellfish.

Uneasy, she walked over to the window and stared onto the rooftops outside.

'Don't wait for me, Marco.'

He watched her, her hand brushing the leaves of the pot-plants, and answered with what he hoped was a tone of straightforward, innocent curiosity. 'Why do you say that?'

'Because you are.'

'I am what?'

'You're waiting for me, Marco. Don't.'

There, she'd said it. Marco's head was bowed in the silence that followed. Lucy sat at the table again, and this time spoke very gently. 'You are, you know. And you really shouldn't.'

He nodded, still looking down. It seemed as if he was never going to speak to her again as he sat tracing the patterns of the tablecloth with his fingers. But when he was finished he looked up, smiling.

'But you like me a little.'

Lucy smiled briefly, for the first time all morning.

'Yes. I like you,' she said, lingering on the word 'like'.

'Then allow me to wait? A little?' he added, almost laughing, but dropping it. 'What's the matter, Lucy?'

'Nothing.'

He shook his head slowly, then reached out and suddenly stroked her forehead.

'Don't!' she cried out, recoiling from his touch. She sat still for a moment in the silence that followed before saying, 'Sorry. I'm sorry, Marco.' Why is it always so? she thought. Why do we always end up screaming at the ones we turn to? And, as soon as she asked herself the question, the memory of the difficult daughter returned, the sound of a flyscreen door slamming in the night, and the assumption that there was all the time in the world to set things right. She suddenly reached out and took his hand. 'I'm sorry. I didn't mean to jump.'

Marco stared back at her, and Lucy was convinced he knew it all. Fortuny, he seemed to say. Fortuny. That was all, no need to say more. He understood. He saw more than she imagined. They were the same age, Marco and Lucy. Yet he seemed wiser to her now than she could ever imagine herself being. She'd jumped and yelled at him like a schoolgirl who didn't know what was happening to her or what she was doing. But she wasn't a schoolgirl and she no longer had that excuse. Marco was calm, he was knowing. At this moment, he gave her the eerie impression of knowing her better than she knew herself, and it suddenly occurred to her that, perhaps, she hadn't been looking. That she'd seen, but she hadn't been looking. And that half acknowledged, passing thought *I'll see Marco tonight* fell into place.

At that moment Marco released his hand from hers and returned to the manuscripts on the floor.

'"Volare."' He smiled, the word bursting from him. 'Everybody loves a good cliché. You should be less— what is the word?—snobby about these things. They're not silly, these songs, they're very good. Nifty.' He grinned. 'We don't have a word like nifty. You are very lucky, you have such words, eh? God, I love English. Have I told you that?'

It was then that Lucy burst out laughing and Marco dropped the sheet music onto the floor beside him, the additions, he informed her, to their list. He picked up another. '"The Baby Elephant Walk", it's a cha-cha.' And he giggled, snapping his fingers rhythmically. 'Cha-cha-cha. Where do these words come from? And then he held up another, his eyes alight. '"Take Five". My favourite.'

'No,' she said, '*mine.*'

'Yours? Do you own it?'

'Yes, and you can't have it. It's *my* favourite. I can play it with my eyes closed.'

And just to demonstrate the point she went straight to Marco's old upright piano, leaned over the keyboard, closed her eyes, and launched into a song that instantly retrieved the girl who was yet to be roused from the sleep of innocence, who'd never heard of Fortuny or sad music, and who played for fun. Only when she'd finished did she open her eyes and look at Marco, triumphantly, as if to say, *There!*

What was happening? What, indeed, was happening? She was twenty-three, and for the first time since arriving she was giving herself leave to be twenty-three, to play silly pop songs that weren't so silly after all. When, she suddenly asked herself, when was the last time she'd had fun? And as she looked back over the years that had brought her here, as she surveyed the whole decade, the time between being thirteen and twenty-three, she remembered only the work, the hours and hours of practice, day in and day out, and suddenly it seemed the emptiest of decades. Astonishingly, it now seemed to her, she had forgotten to live.

Within an hour they had revised their list and agreed to run through the numbers the next day. It would be easy, said Marco, smiling. They were just silly pop songs after all. Lucy laughed, and left.

As Marco watched her go, his face was serious. Lucy had been nervy, distracted, sad. Not her usual self. She was, he thought, in something over her head. He watched her long strides taking her across the small square below him, noting again, with a half-smile, that at least she was tall. He returned to the table, the room, the view from the window, the bright summer flowers, the sheets of music over the floor, the piano: all part of the morning they'd shared, but which was now done; and all redolent of an atmosphere that came when something was over.

Irrelevant houses, shops, cafés, hotels and institutions of public significance, filled with their fraught irrelevant lives, all floated by like so many painted scenes along a gallery wall as Fortuny wove his way through the tiny calles of San Polo. Children squabbled, tourists quibbled, students lingered in doorways or sat reading in open, sunny squares. But none of it mattered. Not to Fortuny. Fortuny was in love.

For the first time in a year he had woken that morning without asking himself, 'How do I feel?' or 'What shall I do with the day?' Since he'd ceased being Paolo Fortuny, Artist, Fortuny, El Maestro, that was a question he'd asked himself every morning: how could he fill his days? Now he was elevated by unexpected love, floating above it all. Love, the miraculous convergence of two lost halves, was the only answer Fortuny had ever required and the effect of its magic was instantaneous. And as he paused on a small bridge to take his bearings, he carried with him the deeply thrilling knowledge that Lucy was just out there, not more than a mile away, doing something at that very moment.

It was an occasion to be marked with an appropriate sense of ceremony, but there was a problem: the only place fit to celebrate such a momentous event was fully booked. It was extraordinary. First thing that morning Fortuny had instructed Rosa to make the reservation, only to be told a few moments later that there was no place for Signor Fortuny and his guest. Not that evening, or the one after. There was, of course, some mistake, and he would have to rectify it himself.

Fortuny stepped off the small bridge, cleared a path through the cluttered lane and finally rapped on the glass restaurant door. The staff were sympathetic, apologised profusely, but, no, there was no mistake. There was simply not a table available that night. Times had changed in the year since Signor Fortuny had last dined there. The restaurant had acquired a wide public fame now, and Signor Fortuny would, of course, be aware of the advantages and disadvantages of fame. Patrons now booked in advance from as far away as New York.

The situation looked hopeless until Fortuny ventured to suggest that a small space could be created by the bar where the dessert trolley now sat. A small table would fit there quite nicely, would it not? It was an unusual request, of course, but could this not be done, if not out of good business sense, then for old times' sake?

The owner raised his eyebrows and looked at the head waiter, who shrugged his shoulders and threw the

problem back to the owner. In the silence that followed, Fortuny reached for his wallet and was about
to produce a number of large notes when the owner
stopped him. 'Please,' he muttered, waving the money
away, 'Signor Fortuny, please.'

He then beckoned a waiter, issued his instructions,
and Fortuny watched as a small table for two was created in the exact spot he had suggested. When the task
was completed the owner smiled and bowed to Fortuny, who returned the courtesy. There would be a
table for the Signor and his guest. Indeed, there always
would…

Walking back, oblivious of the crowds, Fortuny
breathed in the luxurious summer air and mentally selected the suit he would wear that evening.

The world was not too exhausted after all, the age
not too tired, to eke out one last miracle. As he crossed
the Campo San Polo it occurred to Fortuny, that, at
sixty-three, he might now be worthy enough not only
to receive the blessing of love but to give it as well. It
even occurred to him that he might very well be really
in love for the first time.

At home, in the salon, his eyes lit on his cello, and lingered—lingered neither with regret nor with the
empty feeling that the instrument had so often
brought out in him recently. No, when he looked at it
now, this morning, he was young again. He was per-

forming once more; he was the Fortuny who had stared back at the camera with moody eyes that hot summer in Rome years before. He was on stage, breathing in the rarefied air, savouring the hush before the music began. For to stand on the stage of a concert hall, bow in hand, was to stand on a mountain-top and survey the outstretched landscape of the audience below. Not that he even needed to open his eyes to know they were there. He could feel them, the members of the audience, out there, huddled in silence, waiting. And then the sound suddenly coming from Fortuny's bow and strings, the only sound on earth apart from the small grunts of effort that only he could hear, and the slight hum that he sometimes slipped into when playing, which was occasionally even audible on recordings.

On that night, twenty years ago in Rome, the first concert of a triumphant season that had everybody grappling for new ways in which to couch their praise, he had them in the palm of his hand, as he always did then. And he remembered that feeling now with remarkable immediacy. Remembered how he *knew* he had them from the moment the first of his soon-to-be-famous earthy notes was slapped into life, and the whole house went still and quiet, not simply listening to a concert but witnessing an event. As much as anything, it was the sheer energy, the physical force, the all-conquering will of the player, that silenced them, for—to Fortuny—performance was, above all, the imposition of the self on all those gathered to listen. Will, energy, strength and that something extra that no one else had. It was all of that, channelled with unquestioned confidence into the hands, through the fingertips to the strings, to produce the saddest of music, that stunned the house into stillness and silence.

That was the Fortuny of those years, the Fortuny who fed off the silent tribute, who knew no nerves, who gathered together the sum parts of his self, and silenced the house. And no concert did he ever consider a success unless he could feel that silence and know he had prevailed. The sweat flying from his forehead as he tossed his head back or flung it from side to side, his humming often rising with the music; the women in the front rows, wincing and starting with every slap of the bow as if being struck themselves. Such was the Fortuny of those years, and it was all part of the conquest, as were the little tricks (which he now passed on to Lucy), the intricacies, the movements, the runs, so subtly and swiftly executed that they seemed effortless. And, indeed, were.

Fortuny, standing in his salon here and now, but also standing on that long-ago stage in Rome, listens to the last note of that concert fade, his shirt drenched, hair dripping, mind and body drained, then looks up and takes it in, that sudden, oceanic roar as the house breaks its silence. And, as the remembered sound of that ovation envelops him, he knows that he was never so alive as he was at such moments.

Chapter Eleven

IN HER flat Lucy could hear once again the low, the guttural sounds of that lost language Fortuny had retrieved the night before. Throughout the day it had seemed like the stuff of somebody else's memories, somebody else's dream, but as evening rolled in, she began to feel, once again, its pull. The pull of a strange, elemental sound that seemed to have crept from some forgotten corner of history just for her. And with that came Fortuny's voice. Rolling, almost rumbling towards her, like the deep notes and the sharp jabs of his music.

And as she relived those sensations, she caught a glimpse of that other Lucy, for this wave that was Fortuny and was rolling towards her could also drown her. And when the wave broke over her and she felt its full weight, she would become that other Lucy—forever—living in the shadow of Fortuny, drawn into the house of Fortuny, gradually losing herself in its many hallways and its rooms that led to other rooms, which opened out onto more rooms, each of which had witnessed century upon century of young brides and mistresses who had entered the house—entered, and bowed to its will until they eventually forgot who they once were. And why not her? Could she not become his eternal companion, his eternal understudy, the young mistress who filled the house with the laughter and youthful sounds it now lacked, until it became her life and she forgot who she'd once been? It was a snapshot of a life glimpsed in an instant, a preview of what might be…

Need it really be like that? She could see another Lucy: too young for fear, different, wiser than that long line of wives and mistresses who had entered the house young and grown old inside its walls. Yes, she saw another Lucy, wiser and stronger, not condemned to follow the patterns of the past, a young woman who just might dismantle the Fortunys of this world even as she desired them; who could break the iron laws of history by discovering and dissecting the forces that governed them. This Lucy would find her way and never forget who she was, because those days were over.

But which Lucy to follow? Out there in the world, where real lives were played out not in speculation but in fact, there was only one life to choose, one life waiting—no possibility of recasting the years. In life there were no sneak previews, no way of knowing just what might happen, or how it would feel if such and such were ever set in motion. A whole life could turn on a single choice, just as it could change upon hearing a single strain of music.

She lowered the deep, red dress over her, that dress with a cut, a colour and a feel like nothing else she'd ever known. The first time she'd worn it had been because Fortuny had dropped it over her shoulders and draped her in it before she'd known what was happening. But she knew now. As she watched the shadows falling across the walls outside, eyed the washing hanging from lines, and saw the old lady opposite leaning out of her window, Lucy felt once more the pull of that strange, sad language, knowing full well that it had travelled across oceans, over fields and over the years, just to be here.

It was a small restaurant but, Fortuny explained to Lucy, famous. So were those who dined here: with a sweep of his hand, he indicated the far wall lined with framed photographs of celebrities. Naturally, they included a portrait of him, a brooding Fortuny, taken, Lucy now knew, one hot and irritable summer morning in 1962.

When they arrived, he introduced her to the owner and the head waiter, both of whom he addressed by their first names. This, he said, is Lucia, and they smiled. They could tell from his manner that he was happy, and that this Signorina Lucia beside him was the source. And Lucy was pleased for Fortuny, even though she felt an uncomfortable sense of being not so much introduced as displayed. She was reminded of those middle-aged businessmen she'd met at extended family functions at home, proudly presenting their young wives. Yes, she thought, Fortuny seemed to be flaunting her, like they had flaunted their beautiful young wives. Beauty, she could hear the voice of her school friend Sally Happer saying, marries money and together they have beautiful children.

Now Fortuny was fussing, only had eyes for her. And perhaps, she reflected, that was the beginning and end of it. He was happy, that was all. Did she like the wine? The place? Rhetorical questions, for they were impossible to dislike and Fortuny barely paused for an answer. The restaurant had, he went on, been a well-guarded secret for years until an American journalist had written about it in the *New York Times*. Now you had to book, perhaps a week in advance.

In fact, when Fortuny had telephoned Lucy that afternoon, asking how she had slept and informing her that he had slept the deep sleep of a man half his age, he had also told her that he had been fortunate enough to arrange a free table at a special restaurant; told her how lucky they were because the establishment was so famous, so popular. But, he'd said, his laughter rippling into her ears, the gods had created a table for them. With the cha-cha rhythms of 'The Baby Elephant

Walk' still in her ears, she had agreed to go, but had had second thoughts from the moment she'd put the phone down and noted the faintest trace of the previous night's grappa still on her tongue.

And now he was fussing, and they were drawing amused stares of which he was completely oblivious because all could see was Lucy. Did she need anything else? The fine Colombian coffee they served? Cake? Amoretti biscuits? No, she didn't want any of them.

'That's just as well.' Fortuny sipped his wine. 'Rosa has left wafers and wine out for us.' He then put his empty glass down, decisively, implying that the course of the evening was already decided. But not by anybody in particular. The whole day, in fact, had simply fallen into place of its own accord. And now the wafers and the wine awaited their moment in the order of things.

Lucy's shoes clipped along the marble floor of the now dimly lit *portego*. At first she had looked for the chocolates, the wafers and wine in the salon, but, without a word, he had taken her hand and now led her along the *portego*, past the lines of family portraits which, as well being indistinct in the dim light, suddenly seemed gloomy to Lucy. At the top of the *portego* they turned into a sitting room where she recognised the scratchy dark mirror in a gilded frame, in which in which she had once secretly caught the reflection of Fortuny mi-

micking Fortuny. She was staring up at the sky-blue ceiling, the usual sportive angels and cherubs, when Fortuny touched her shoulder and she turned to find herself staring along a row of opened doors. Two, three, four of them, ending with a dull circle of light on the carpeted floor of what could only be Fortuny's bedroom.

Wondering where the space for all these rooms could possibly come from, Lucy followed her white-suited host through that succession of opened doors that led from room to room, each of them a subtle variation on the others. And all the time she had an uneasy feeling that she had fallen in with the design of things, with this little ritual, and all the other rituals, big and small and unnoticed, that might await her. At the same time she was aware that not just nights, but years, could pass like that, and that speculative glimpse of a life unlived in which a young woman forgot who she once was could well come true. But throughout the walk, some forty metres, her eyes remained focused on the open door at the end. They passed another sitting room, a tea room, the former bedroom of Fortuny's late mother and, finally, reached Fortuny's own bedroom.

The room was softly lit by two lamps in opposite corners. There was a dressing-table and a large oval mirror in the room, a small serving table and, next to one of the lamps, a desk. Fortuny threw his coat on a chair and casually walked towards the serving table, upon which Rosa had indeed left the wine and wafers.

'Ah, dear, dear Rosa,' he said, slapping his hands together and casually lifting the wine bottle to Lucy in enquiry.

Lucy barely noticed. It wasn't a large room, but it was hushed, sparser than she'd thought it would be— if, indeed, she'd thought of it all. The windows were closed behind drawn, full-length, gold-coloured curtains, and long gold-edged hangings covered the walls. The bed, with its tall rococo bedhead, a small cameo Madonna embedded in the centre, was covered in gold pillows and a heavy gold quilt. Everything was gold.

To inhabit Fortuny's bedroom was to inhabit a sealed, timeless chamber in which centuries of the family had been created, a room in which they themselves had procreated and in which they had eventually died. There was no sense of the outside world in this room. No sense of society, or history, other than that of the family. The only sound to intrude was that of the occasional taxi on the canal. To enter the room was to enter a lost corner of an imperial age, a last preserve, the final days and nights of which were disappearing even as she stood there, fading like the last seconds of a dazzling dream.

Fortuny closed the door behind her, shutting it snug against its marble borders, and closing out, for a time, the remorseless, creeping world; closing out, for a time, that inevitable day when tourists would surely walk through that very door and stand in the same room to admire, to sneer, or to grow bored, as they reconstructed the lives that had once been lived inside.

Fortuny raised the wine bottle to Lucy once again and this time she nodded, watching as he filled the glass with the bubbling Prosecco. The air was warm, close, and she longed to throw the windows open. In the quiet solemnity of the room, she suddenly kicked her sandals off as she emptied her glass in one, long draught and passed it back to Fortuny, who refilled it, smiling, enchanted, as he sipped from his own. The sparkling wine, Lucy noted, was as invigorating as diving off the rocks into the fizzing waves of the beaches of her youth and, as she lowered the glass again, she pushed her fingers through Fortuny's hair. His face was hidden in half-shade, his eyes in shadow, and once again he was *her* Fortuny. And in a moment of deliberate irreverence, she raised her dress over her head and threw it on the floor, quickly following with her underclothes, which seemed to flutter through the air, delighting him.

But it wasn't just the desire for irreverence that had spurred Lucy: it was also a response to some need in her that wanted it all to be done *now*. She needed, in some part of her, to see the thing through. Now. This she realised only later—at that moment, the need was only half perceived, half conceded, as she pursued the inevitable course of the night.

From the heavy gold quilt of the bed she looked about the room, at the Madonna above her head, the cupids and winged women at sport in the clouds. She noted the ever-present family portraits and the shiny surface of the walnut writing desk, looking for all the world as if it had never had a word written from it, and glanced at the locked door, solid and heavy like that of a crypt. Fortuny was moving towards one of the lamps when Lucy suddenly spoke.

'Leave it.'

He turned, surprised, alarmed at her tone, but she repeated herself.

'I want to see the room. Please, leave the light.'

Reluctantly, he complied, and came towards the bed, where he stood and removed his tie, unbuttoned his cream cotton shirt and, after folding it carefully, placed it on a small armchair beside him. With his singlet removed, Lucy saw the leanness of Fortuny's body, the solidity of his forearms, and the strength in the shoulders and upper arms that had come from a lifetime of performance. His curly body hair was grey, betraying his age, but his physique was that of a man who still looked after himself, who had not let himself run to flab. Who had, she mused, been somewhere extraordinary…

But she was also conscious of the fact that his eyes

were lowered and that he hadn't looked up since beginning this awkward business of undressing in front of a woman for—she guessed—the first time in a long time. And suddenly she was oddly moved, a little sad, and wanted to say something light and amusing. Something reassuring and comforting. Then, as he lowered his white cotton trousers, she almost laughed at what she saw: there, hanging below the border of his silk, sky-blue underpants, was Fortuny's left testicle. Ponderous, pendulous, white, hairless; as round and smooth as a pebble in a stream.

She looked away in case she really did laugh, and when she looked back Fortuny was above her. He hummed softly in her ear, in that strange and distant language of his city, but, intriguing though it was to hear it all again, and as much as she felt its pull, she *was* hearing it for the second time, and already it was beginning to lose its power, to feel like a well-practised part of a well-practised lover's repertoire. And even as he caressed her neck, her arms and her body with his practised hands, and even as she surrendered to them, those hands, those fingers of Fortuny, were no longer those of the unreachable, untouchable Maestro, the dark, commanding figure on a mountaintop surveying all beneath him. This was that other Fortuny, resurrecting the old tricks that had always worked with the ladies in the past.

Now, as she pushed his silver hair away, she kissed

his forehead and, in the low light of the room, found herself staring directly into the blue of Fortuny's eyes, into the pale eyes of the Maestro. Those brooding eyes that, for so long, had stared back at her only through shadow and time, but which were now no more than an inch away. And for a moment, but only a moment, Fortuny caught that stare and quickly turned aside.

It was a stare, Fortuny concluded, long and disarmingly direct, that seemed to be searching, scouring his eyes for something that lay hidden. But what? This young woman had studied him from a distance all her life and, it seemed, she was studying him still. Still observing. Hers was the stare of one of those fabulous creatures, those confident young women one saw on the streets, who gave every impression of being able to dismantle you even as they desired you. Youth. And at that point he closed his eyes, turned away, and buried himself in the perfume of her hair. The same hair she had shaken free on his salon floor when she had performed that simple, utterly unselfconscious act that had wrenched him from the dead past, from the age that had existed before he'd ever known this Lucia, and into the luminous present.

From that moment on, Fortuny was her prisoner, doomed to wait upon her with the anxious, adolescent heart of first love. He was a happy prisoner, happy to mark and define his days by the presence, or absence, of his Lucia. For this young woman, he felt sure, could do anything. She could conquer anybody the way she had conquered him, perform magic and miracles and revive legions of emotions he'd long thought dead and buried. She could thicken the blood in his veins and grant him another lifetime altogether, another age.

As Fortuny experienced his second orgasm in less than twenty-four hours, and as he became aware of Lucy's arms closing around him in the hush of his room, he felt, for all the world, as if that age was just beginning.

One perfect smoke ring followed another. Fortuny, now wrapped in a blue silk dressing-gown, the family insignia on its lapel, sat in the armchair beside the table that held the wafers and wine. The Prosecco, he noticed, was still fresh. Another perfect circle floated across the room. He sat, sipping his Prosecco, entranced by the spectacle of this young woman who could perform such wonders as smoke rings.

But as he lifted his eyes to the ceiling he didn't see how Lucy, lounging under the gold quilt of the bed, suddenly stabbed the cigarette into the ashtray and automatically lit another. All Fortuny saw was the wonder of a perfect smoke ring, floating over the bed, the marble floor, and dissolving into the far wall of his bedroom. Finally, he broke the silence, raising his glass in toast and taking a wafer from the tray.

'Dear Rosa,' he said, eyeing the table. 'Dear, thoughtful Rosa.'

But Lucy, who had drunk rather more of the wine than she had intended, responded fiercely, 'She doesn't like me.'

Fortuny swung to face her, genuinely surprised. 'Rosa?'

'Yes, Rosa. In fact, she hates me.'

He laughed. 'Oh, Lucia, Rosa doesn't hate anybody.'

Fortuny laughed again at the thought, while Lucy suddenly launched another wonder into the air. Everything—the sudden oppressive heat of the room, the house, the talk, his laughter—was growing intolerable. Her transformation from Lucy to Lucia was now merely annoying. She wasn't Lucia, she was Lucy. But this, she could see with instant clarity, was the way it would be. Just as he'd smoothed her rough edges and taught her his subtleties, he would mould her into his Lucia. And she thought of the red dress and saw it through Marco's eyes. She had draped herself in it tonight, not so much out of affection for Fortuny but, she was now realising, as a parting gesture. The dress, the Lucias, the tiresome subtlety, the lectures, the 'one simply knows' and the 'one simply sees', were now weighing on her like a costume she could never comfortably wear and which she was impatient to shrug off. For this would be it, this would be the way of the house—the House of Fortuny—and this would be the way the years would roll out before her, until whatever she had been before would fade to a dot, then disappear. Until she simply gave in and *was* Lucia.

This time Fortuny saw the swift, sudden motion of Lucy jabbing the half-smoked cigarette into the ashtray, as she repeated, 'Well, she hates me. And if you don't know why, you're blind.'

With that, she swivelled from the bed, hit the floor in one swift movement, and threw the dress over her shoulders as if it were a mere trifle of a thing. Fortuny barely had time to put his glass back on the table.

'What are you doing?'

As Lucy smoothed the skirt of the dress, she gave him an almost contemptuous look as if to say, *Surely it's perfectly obvious.*

'I'm going.' She slipped into her sandals and threw her hair back. Fortuny was helpless to stop her.

'But why?'

She sighed ever so slightly, crossed the floor and stopped beside him, her hand on his shoulder, her tone quieter.

'Paolo.' She smiled, suddenly tender again, suddenly sixteen, tossed by forces she barely understood, transported back to a time when she had barely grasped what was happening to her or why. She placed her arms around him, and kissed him. Kissed him—it occurred to her much later—not so much to say goodnight as goodbye.

'It's late. I have much to do.'

Then, with Fortuny perhaps even contemplating the nature of that kiss, Lucy wet her fingers and closed the lids of his eyes in the same way she had done the previous evening. But this time, instead of remaining closed, they sprang open again, suddenly wide, frightened, panicked; the eyes of a marionette, lurching to invisible strings and sensing that those strings might suddenly be severed.

Lucy leapt back. At least, she tried to leap back, but Fortuny's fingers were firmly clasped about her wrist, his hands—workman's hands—surprisingly powerful. She remembered how he had slammed the piano lid shut when they'd fought; how the action had carried a hint of violence, even (she'd thought at the time) carried with it the shadow of a thug. And she suddenly remembered Marco's warnings, that she was getting in over her head, that these people were not to be messed with, and for a moment—but only a moment—she felt frightened. Then it was gone, as Fortuny's grip relaxed. They were, after all, Fortuny's playing hands. And his music, those rasping tones that had once roused her from sleep, passed through her again as she watched, then felt, Fortuny's lips kissing her fingers, cupping them as if they were a gift of rare tropical fruit and the court of his senses was receiving their delights.

In the silence, under the still glow of the lamps and the steady eyes of the multiplicity of shadowy ancestors that crowded the walls, Lucy slowly withdrew her hand.

Fortuny watched her as her fingers slipped from his hand, looked around the room now redolent of unfulfilled promise and, reluctantly, said, 'If you must go… then I suppose you must, my dear Lucy.'

Lucy nodded. Yes, the nod said, yes, she must. But her eyes, lingering on this, her melancholy maestro, held a hint of another story, one that suggested she just might stay after all.

And it was then that Fortuny, utterly unaware of his mistake, said the worst possible thing he could have said at that moment. It was a casual remark, tender in its delivery, but for Lucy his words opened the door on Fortuny past, present and future.

'You are impetuous.' He smiled, gently stroking her cheek as he spoke. 'If I could just put some sense into that little head of yours.'

What surprised Lucy most of all was not so much the remark as how she reacted to it. She was, in her silence, she noted, being understanding of Fortuny— understood that, in the language of the day, this was what was called a 'generational moment'. And she acknowledged the truth of that even as she laughed at the language itself. She realised fully for the first time that her very understanding of him now placed her beyond his field of gravity. And no amount of sad music or lost dialect could make her feel his pull again. And just then, as Fortuny's hand fell from her cheek, she could have sworn she heard the thud of some dead weight landing at her feet.

Chapter Twelve

SHE was light, she was weightless. Leaving Fortuny's, floating over the courtyard stones, Lucy heard the whispered voices in her head—Marco's voice, Sally Happer's, her dead mother's—trailing after her in the hot, scented air, enquiring if she were drinking the water or the wave…

And at that moment the Fortuny that had been the hidden face of her adolescence began to fade like a photographic development in reverse, dissolve into a cloudy solution, returning to nothing, not even the past. The image, tapering to a single white dot of consciousness, then disappearing, ending, as it was always going to. Only the image of the Fortuny she had just left remained to her. *Her* Fortuny was finally gone. For when dreams that have been lived come to an end, they do so quickly, indifferent to the dreamer and the dream. And when they have gone, you open your eyes and see things clearly, possibly for the first time. You have been deceived: it was only a dream.

And so Lucy stood in Fortuny's courtyard, looking

about her as if having woken at last from a decade-long dream, the thing that had brought her across oceans, over fields and over the years. Left the shadowy image of a twilight god, the most enchanting of myths, now obliterated by the bright, hard lights of the courtyard and the empty squares she crossed on the winding path back to her flat.

The next day Fortuny telephoned, leaving a message, but she did not return the call. Later in the afternoon, while she made her way to Marco's flat to rehearse those little songs he'd selected, he telephoned again, a hint of concern in his voice, but again she did not reply. She reprimanded herself for ignoring him, a nagging voice going round and round in her head that said, I thought you were better than that, but you're petty after all. And cowardly. Aren't you? A message could be ignored (at least for some time), but the reality of what had taken place couldn't. If only he'd just go away now, fade like a photograph in the sun. How convenient that would be...

But even as Lucy allowed the thought, she disowned it. That wasn't her, surely? That was some other Lucy. But there was no one else in the room, just this girl who couldn't go on wishing reality away forever, never returning calls. And then the inevitable—and point-less—thought came to her, as it was always going to: if only she'd left it all well enough alone. If only she'd kept Fortuny as a plaything, a toy to be taken out and put away at will. She would always have known him, revered him, dreamed of him, but from a distance only. And he would never have known her at all. Now, this way, at the end of it all, somebody's heart was always bound to break.

She would, of course, see him again. At least once. But not just yet. Not this afternoon and not tonight. Tonight the student trio—Marco, herself and their colleague Guillermo—were playing in the square, and a faint, sad smile lit her features as the rhythms of the cha-cha and all those nifty little tunes Marco had found returned to her.

And, in spite of herself, this jumble of responses that was Lucy suddenly burst into a giggle at the way Marco savoured words. The way he said, 'God, I love English,' with just that right balance of irony and sincerity. Why hadn't she been looking? But even as she asked herself she knew, and the giggle tapered off into silence as she crossed the Giudecca.

How do these things come about? How is it that within six months, and in all the years that would follow, the sight, the very thought even, of a five-pound note could be enough to bring her to the point of tears?

They were sitting in Marco's flat, lit up by the afternoon sun, going over the songs for that night, when

Lucy suddenly tired of them and, without warning, broke into a piece of Elgar. She sank into the music as if sinking into a warm bath in which she might forget herself, forget everything, and she thought she *had* lost herself completely in it when a sudden run of high, rapidly descending notes floated over her music and fell on her without warning. It was like being dive-bombed by swallows. She looked up to see Marco not even looking at his violin but staring out over the rooftops as he improvised, playing completely by ear. She dropped her head immediately, attacking her cello, filling the room with sharp, rasping notes, followed by a long, drawn-out ache of a sound as the notes almost slid, collapsing into each other. And she'd no sooner completed this progression when he swept down on her again, a rush of notes darting in and out of hers, changing the whole composition so that she forgot all about Elgar and was simply improvising with Marco.

Over the next twenty, or even thirty, minutes—they were completely unaware of time—they attacked and counter-attacked, sometimes harmonising, their flocks of notes touching, brushing against each other, in mid-air it seemed, and blending together before suddenly breaking away and veering off each on their own course. One moment they'd be playing separate pieces entirely, each shunning the other, the next throwing themselves back to collide note upon note, almost creating a smacking sound in the air. Lucy's hair came loose from its band, Marco's fringe had fallen over his face. Their jerked attempts to toss the hair from their eyes failed as they dug deep into the music. This music, which was like nothing Lucy had ever played or even imagined she could play: at once in harmony and opposition, advancing and retreating, flirting and dismissive, solemn and flighty, tender and cruel, certain and confused. All that, and more.

And when they finally stopped, both of them completely played out and exhausted, and looked up into each other's faces, hair everywhere, brows and hands sweaty and sticky, and eyes still wild, they suddenly burst into laughter, exhausted, delirious laughter, as though asking each other how that had started, where it had come from, and what it meant—while, all the time, each knew full well where it had come from and what it meant.

Their laughter slowly subsided and, although the notes had faded, the memory of them persisted, as if still hanging in the air. Lucy rested her bow against her chair, Marco placed his violin on the table and inclined his head, bowing to her. The gesture was more than a compliment—it was the recognition of an artistic equal, or perhaps more. She returned the nod, a reciprocal recognition of his mastery, sincerely meant. His playing was exhilarating, as exciting as everybody said it could be, but until now she'd never really heard him set his fingers free. His eyes lit up and he looked directly at her.

'A bet?' he said, then paused. 'What do you call it? A wager?'

Lucy grinned. 'About what?'

'Us.'

'What about us?'

He paused again, like a raconteur savouring his punch line before delivering it.

'The first to achieve success.' And he was laughing again, his delivery, once more, just the right balance of irony and sincerity. 'Let us say…newspaper success? The first one receives from the other an English five-pound note. It may,' he went on, 'be delivered personally by hand, or posted. As the case may be.'

'An English five-pound note?'

'Yes.'

'Why a five-pound note?'

'I don't know—does it matter?'

'No.'

He leaned forward. 'Bet?'

'Bet.'

She then reached out her hand, still clammy from playing, and they shook on the deal. Their eyes were smiling, it was all good fun, but she was aware that they held the handshake just that bit longer than social convention deemed necessary. And when they withdrew, she smiled inwardly at the convention, the strange logic, of granting people permission to touch.

While walking back to her flat for a short break before setting off to play in the square that evening, she thought again of that sudden outbreak of sound, that outburst of notes that could never be assembled again. Then she smiled to herself about their wager, little realising that the sight, the very idea of a five-pound note, would one day be enough to bring her to the point of tears.

That evening Fortuny, assuming that Lucy had been too caught up to call, gave up on the telephone and stopped by the open-air café in St Mark's Square, where he knew she sometimes played. She might not have been there, of course, but she was, and suddenly all was well again. It was a hot night, the square was crowded and he knew he could watch from a far table without being seen himself, for he had no intention of disturbing her. Lucy, he was surprised to see, was at the piano. She was wearing a smart white dress he hadn't seen before and part of him—the first tremor of jealousy—wondered whether she had chosen it herself, or who else might have chosen it for her. As she played she stared ahead in the direction of Florian's, while from the safety of the crowded square Fortuny sat, transfixed, the blood aching in his veins. Not even when he reached for his glass of wine did Fortuny take his eyes off his Lucia.

And he was genuinely impressed with the quality of her jazz piano; her rhythms and timing had the touch of a natural. This was especially true when, more hunched at the piano than she really should have been, she performed the quite complex modern jazz of 'Take Five' with astonishing ease and relish. Fortuny felt himself in a position to judge. He was not only familiar with the music of Mr Dave Brubeck, but with the man himself. Extraordinarily, he had once shared a stage with him, and had written to him afterwards saying how much he admired his handling of the 9/8, 4/4 rhythms of 'Blue Rondo à la Turk'—one of his favourites. This had, in fact, led to an irregular but extended correspondence between the two men, and Fortuny made a mental note to mention the matter to Lucy when next he was with her. When—and he mulled over the phrase as the ache returned to his veins—next he was with her.

During the break he watched as she sat down with the accordionist and the violinist, a young man he had seen at the Conservatorium and of whom big things were expected. At one point the young violinist attempted a clumsy, but nonetheless affectionate gesture. He had been eating chocolates, and had attempted to share one with Lucy by popping it into her mouth as she laughed at something he had told her. But the chocolate missed Lucy's mouth, landing on the ground, and Fortuny saw, or thought he saw, Lucy brushing the boy's hand away. He smiled inwardly, more than content at this. What he didn't see, however, was that, in fact, Lucy had reached for Marco's hand in an attempt to better guide the chocolate to her lips, and between them they had bungled the move.

When the trio began playing again, Lucy on the cello now, Fortuny left the square as invisibly as he had arrived. He had longed to speak to Lucy but hadn't wished to create a stir. While he walked home, the incident involving Lucy, the young man and the uneaten chocolate replayed itself in his mind. The incident had soothed him. He had been pleased, heartened, encouraged by her dismissal of the young violinist, who had clearly made a playful but clumsy advance and she had dismissed him. This was good. And when he next saw Lucy he would compliment her on her piano-playing... There was at least something of a slight spring in Fortuny's step, a resonant ring as his metalled heels hit the stones of the tiny, familiar laneway.

But the episode had also unsettled him: that young man so close to his Lucia's laughing lips, the tips of his fingers so near before she'd brushed them away. Above all, though, the image Fortuny carried home with him that night was that of Lucy playing. Lucy lost in the world of playing, of performing: a world, Fortuny knew full well, that was self-enclosed, sealed. She was a born performer, he was convinced of that. And she was already stirring interest in the town.

Recently she had played at a recital with a string quartet in the Scuola di San Rocco. A large crowd had been seated in the upper hall of the building, and again Fortuny had been one of many, deliberately seated at the back of the hall. He preferred it that way, for Lucy had not told him of the recital. He had only found out about it from a poster, and had assumed her reticence was due to modesty, or even nervousness.

But there were no nerves in her playing. She was too young for nerves and her playing was, he confessed, exciting. Then, when the quartet had finished, Fortuny watched from the back of the hall as the audience rose and a bald-headed man with a face like a frog threw his arms around Lucy and planted his slippery lips on her cheek. This Bellini, Fortuny sneered. What does he know? Lucy was *his*, Fortuny's, student, and the excitement of her playing came from the knowledge, the skills and tricks that *he* had passed on to her. Not this Bellini. Yet there the man was, slobbering over her as if he'd had anything to do with it!

Fortuny kicked the stones beneath his feet as he turned into the small calle that led to his courtyard door. She had not told him of the recital and he had left unobserved that night as he had this evening. Perhaps he would raise the matter in the morning when Lucy arrived for her class.

The interior of the small hotel glowed at the bottom of the street. The smiling eyes of the concierge and the indifferent air of the plump cat greeted the Maestro as he passed. It was late, but he noted from the courtyard that Rosa's light was still on.

* * *

The next day Lucy's flat was stuffy, the air hot. She stepped out onto the street to clear her head and meandered, without noticing where she was going, down through the winding lanes of San Polo and Dorsoduro, skirting the crowds. When she finally stopped to catch her bearings, she realised she was standing in front of the Accademia bridge: she had blundered into Fortuny's territory. She quickly crossed the bridge, then the square and took the first lane she came to, again wandering aimlessly until she came to a specialist stationery store beside a quiet canal. She paused to look at the prints in the window, admired the hand-made envelopes and aquatints, and contemplated buying a set of postcards for her father. They were old-world drawings of the city, pressed into the paper in a variety of colours, and while she was studying them she became distantly aware of a door closing and a figure standing beside her.

'Lucia!'

Lucy tried to smile.

'Paolo.'

She had contemplated Fortuny, even Signor Fortuny, but, of course, that would have been absurd in the circumstances. There was no going back to the restraint and formality they'd known before they'd crossed the divide between restraint and release.

'Forgive me, Paolo. I've meant to call you.'

'Are you ill?'

'No.'

She clearly wasn't.

'Then why?'

'Why what?'

'Why are you avoiding me?'

Lucy shook her head, but it was useless. Fortuny clicked his tongue, his voice was soft, confidential but firm. Like a parent, Lucy couldn't help but notice.

'We're not children.'

'No.' Lucy tried to avoid his stare. 'We're not.'

'Then why are you behaving childishly?'

His voice had risen and he looked about the street, annoyed with himself.

Lucy, knowing full well the reason for his annoyance and wondering just how she had bungled into his territory, was thrown and confused by their sudden meeting. She found herself lapsing into the very formality she'd just deemed irretrievably dead.

'Please, Signor Fortuny…'

'Paolo, please,' he muttered. 'This formality is absurd.'

She then turned this way and that, as if lost, and was about to excuse herself when Fortuny's hand—the hand that only a few days before had clasped hers and kissed her fingers—grabbed her wrist.

'Lucia.' His voice was softer. 'Tomorrow, please come to dinner.'

'Dinner?'

'Please.'

'Oh, Paolo,' she said. 'Paolo, that's very kind of you, but…'

Fortuny looked at her intently. 'You're jumpy,' he said.

'Am I?'

He stared into her eyes, fixed her with his gaze, then continued, a pleading note entering his voice.

'One night, dear Lucia, just one night. It would make me very happy. And perhaps you, also. And Rosa. She would love to prepare something special, she has so little opportunity.'

Lucy tried to turn away from him, but he was still gripping her wrist and passers-by were beginning to pay attention to the spectacle of the young woman and the older man quite clearly engaged in a strained conversation. Somebody in the crowd smirked and a small group paused in front of a café, observing and listening. It was hopeless.

'Yes,' she said. 'Yes. That will be nice.'

Fortuny released his grip, then raised her hand and quickly kissed it.

'Tomorrow, then.'

'I must go, Paolo.' She kissed his cheek and stared at him, signalling the sadness with her eyes, the sadness that just might tell him that the thing has been lived and the thing is over. But he saw only his Lucia, in his eyes a smile.

'Tomorrow.'

Lucy backed away into the slowly flowing crowd, the figure of Fortuny, in his coat and hat, offering her a slight bow as she went. And as she went, she realised his eyes were mooning. Tomorrow… In her jeans and T-shirt she waved goodbye to him, knowing that once she would have crossed oceans, fields and years, to meet Fortuny on that promised tomorrow. As she walked away, the expression on Fortuny's face followed.

She knew that expression, had seen it in the eyes of disappointed suburban lovers in her high-school years, mooning at her through the windscreens of their cars as they'd driven reluctantly away, stirring the gravel of the McBrides' circular driveway. She knew it all right, but had never thought to see it in Fortuny's eyes. Yet there it was. He was hanging on to her. No longer the faraway tumble of notes, the source of the mysterious music that had at first woken, then soothed the younger Lucy. No longer the distant, the most enchanting of myths, the unfathomable artist with the brooding stare. That was all gone. Fortuny was mooning over her.

That night, while Lucy was playing to tourists in the square and losing her thoughts in the lightness of it all, Fortuny stood over the walnut table in his study, once more surveying the whole of his family's history. That history, which read like an epic tale of loss and gain, and more loss… There to be read in a single sweep of the eyes by those familiar with the story. Some of the names were whole books in themselves, some were chapters, others merely footnotes. It was, indeed, a grand narrative, it was history, populated with figures larger than life, and figures that life had barely noticed. And Fortuny felt the weight of that history now, felt the undeniable imperative written into it as he dwelt on the final entry, circling his name and whispering it to the room, to the portraits on the walls, which looked back at him with an air of impatient expectancy.

On Wednesday morning he rose early, throwing back the curtains to let in the day, noting the sun on the canal, the illuminated reds and greens of the hanging baskets. But also, absent-mindedly, noting one of those late summer skies that are already tinged with the soft glow of autumn.

He dressed with the jaunty haste of a young man, reaching for a shirt, bending for shoes, peering into the mirror. Nothing was an effort, and the light breakfast he took before leaving for the market was a delight.

But once breakfast was completed, Fortuny suddenly felt a shadow of gloom. Perhaps Lucy was avoiding him after all, he thought. She said she'd been busy, but perhaps she'd been lying. He shook his head, dismissed the thought as impossible. This day, he told himself, was not made for such thoughts.

He called for Rosa to clear the table. 'Take them

away,' he said, pointing to his breakfast things, but he had snapped at her and, realising it, mumbled the briefest apology. Rosa leaned over the table and quietly removed the plates, knowing that the young foreign woman, who was always going to be trouble, was at the heart of this. The previous night he had complained about his meal, which he had never done before. It was too tough, he'd said, too cool. The temperature of the fish was crucial, it must not happen again.

Now, stooped over the tray, she took the dishes to the kitchen without looking back. When she was gone, Fortuny concentrated on the bright sunshine of the day, the dazzling greens of the leaves and the reds of the flowers in their baskets, dripping water. Surely nothing could go wrong on such a day as this.

For special occasions Fortuny always shopped at the markets. First, the fish market, with its enticing variety of *fruits de mer*. He was always a deliberate, cautious purchaser, but never more so than today. He stood for a long time at a particular stall selecting, then reselecting, various shellfish, discussing them at length with the seller, then buying a small quantity of several different kinds—sea scallops, shrimp, baby crab, oysters. Finally satisfied, he turned away, almost light-headed. It seemed an age since he'd shopped for a special dinner, and the anticipation, the extravagance, the sensation of doing so was almost intoxicating. Nothing, he told himself, must go wrong.

The summer fruits he selected with even greater care than the seafood, testing the grapes, the peaches, the purple figs and the little wild strawberries imported from France. Again he took only small quantities of a range of fruits, intent on selecting the most flavoursome and completely ignoring the shopkeeper's impatience.

His purchases completed, wrapped and carefully stowed in his English Harrods shopping bags, Fortuny strolled back, admiring the day and the play of sunlight on the walls, the windows and canals. Near his house, he stopped at a small confectioner's where he sipped an *espresso* while making his selection of sweetmeats. The shop buzzed with the pleasant sound of the local people, their conversations not only amusing and invigorating but radiating communal familiarity. The sun, the sounds of the streets, the laughter of the shopkeepers, the ring of the cash register, the signs of life's daily pleasures were once again all about him. And he remembered, quietly remarking to himself as he watched it all (and recalling some words of a Signor Graham Greene, one of his favourite novelists), that this was what hope felt like.

Once home again, his purchases safely handed over to Rosa, he sat on the balcony, reading the morning newspaper. He heard the splash of the water taxis on the canal, sounding, he imagined, like dolphins at play, and anticipated the evening ahead, carefully making sure that everything had been provided for.

That evening Fortuny sipped an aperitif in the study, drummed his fingers on the walnut table, then turned and examined his bow tie in the mirror before adjusting his sleeve length; the family insignia was clearly visible on his cufflinks. Once again, he adjusted his tie and gave his cuffs a final tweak, humming to himself. But, at the same time, a faint but unmistakeable voice in his head suggested that he had become that most pathetic of creatures, an aging man impossibly in love with a young girl. It was the devil on his back, whispering in his ear and telling him that he was being taken for a ride. Mermaids didn't exist and Venus was a planet. When was he going to grow up? But he shrugged his shoulders and heard the thing scamper across the room and out the window, into the evening and onto the rooftops, where it belonged.

With time still on his hands as he waited for Lucy's arrival, Fortuny strolled through the salon. He lightly touched the strings of his old cello, and, for the first time in many months, found himself dwelling on the circumstances of his retirement

Had it only been little more than a year? The time between then and now was a different order of time. Until he had retired, time had woken him each morning, ordered, punctilious, brisk. Over the last year, however, it had rapped on his door at the usual hour, but with nothing for him to do. Time continued to call, and Fortuny continued to receive it, but to what end? And what to do through those days that had become increasingly elastic as the year had worn on?

The bolt from the blue had come when Fortuny had been staying with friends in Rome. While there, he had casually called in for a chat with his agent, who had always organised his concerts. The most recent—a modest success, he thought—had taken in Scandinavia and Austria.

It was, in retrospect, inevitable that the day should have been grey and wet, the streets damp and shiny. But Fortuny had been dry under his umbrella, and even now he could recall, quite vividly, standing in the ground-floor doorway that morning, contentedly shaking the raindrops from his umbrella before making his impromptu call for a casual chat.

Anna, his agent, a woman in her mid-fifties, had greeted him and he had spoken lightly of the weather, of the day, of the city traffic.

'All the noise,' he said with a smile.

'I don't notice it,' she replied, but there were no smiles.

There was a pause, and it was then that Fortuny casually ventured an idea for a forthcoming tour. Anna simply dropped her pen on the desk, spoken flatly and, it afterwards seemed to Fortuny, brutally, considering their long association.

'Paolo, I'm sorry, but there will be no more tours. Not from here. Not backed by us.'

The only sounds were the soft whirr of the heating and the rain on the window. Fortuny, stunned into silence, said nothing.

'Perhaps somebody else will handle you, but we can't any longer. It's too expensive. Times change. I'm sorry.'

She was quiet for a moment before adding, softly, 'I *am* sorry, Paolo.'

Fortuny dropped his hat and stared at the window, at the drizzle on the windowpane, at the white walls, as if not having heard. When he was ready he turned back to Anna.

'This is final?'

She nodded firmly. 'I was going to write, Paolo. I didn't expect to see you again so soon.'

'No,' he muttered, looking down, his eyes on the floor as he spoke. 'You are sure?'

'Quite sure.' she said, quietly opening the book in front of her and shaking her head sadly. 'Your last tour, Paolo. It lost badly, as did the one before. And the reviews were mixed. You read them yourself? Some of them are saying you've lost the magic, that your technique seems shaky. I'm sorry, Paolo. *I* know you, but the marketplace doesn't. And the marketplace is merciless. There just aren't enough people coming to hear you any more.'

She leaned back in her chair, already exhausted with the topic, and passed the accounts across the desk for Fortuny to examine. He shook his head, declining the offer. Anna continued, a gentler tone to her voice.

'We've carried two losses, Paolo. Not again. Not a third.'

Again, Fortuny looked at the floor, then looked up, his eyes blank, and spoke as if his words were intended for no one in particular.

'What shall I do?'

Anna paused, eyeing Fortuny not as a client now but as a friend. 'You're sixty-two, Paolo,' she urged warmly. 'Just enjoy your life. You've earned it.'

'This *is* my life!' he cried out, but the words rang hollow in his ears even as despair made a fist in his stomach. Yet he couldn't, in all honesty, pretend to be entirely surprised. For it was like finally being found out, and the feeling of being found out, of having his fears confirmed, was almost a relief. For some while now he had been finding difficulty with the more intricate passages, unable to counteract a stiffness in some of his fingers—even, on occasion, a little pain. A visit to his physician, brief but devastating, had confirmed the onset of arthritis. His doctor had at first offered the technical term, then, as if having given a common bird its exotic Latin name, reverted to everyday garden language. 'What we call arthritis, Paolo. Common as snails.' However, he was warned, in time he would have to abandon the concert platform altogether. Clearly, to his audiences, that time had now come, the effects of his creeping affliction obviously being worse than he had imagined.

Anna said nothing. How many times had she seen it? Talented, intelligent people reaching the end of their careers, but with absolutely no talent for the art of simply living. Indeed, they appeared terrified of life away from the public arena.

It was only when he was standing once more in the ground-floor doorway that he remembered his umbrella. The drizzle was now steady rain, but turning back was impossible. He could never sit in that room again, for, without the word itself having been spoken, Fortuny had retired.

Within the space of twenty minutes, and with no more than a handful of sentences having been exchanged inside the room and a tiny measure of rain having fallen outside, his whole life, that by which he defined himself, Fortuny, Artist, had been obliterated.

And so Fortuny did not return for his umbrella, because he was no longer the Fortuny who had entered that room. He no longer had the credentials to sit there. The umbrella would remain where it was, to be picked up eventually by someone else, after it had stayed unclaimed in the office long enough to be nobody's…

A few weeks later, using the occasion of a fundraising concert at which he was one of several artists taking part, Fortuny played a short piece by Bach and publicly announced his retirement with a grace and wit that he was far from feeling.

Fortuny looked up from contemplating the cello, dusted, shining under the lamplight. He shook his head to expel the vision of that whole damp day which had soaked into the blotting paper of his memory. Then he noticed the time on the old clock near the hall. Spritely time, he thought, time with a spring in its step, time that runs away from you, if you don't keep a close eye on it, because there's so much to do. In the salon mirror he adjusted his tie once again and his spirits lifted as he thought of the night ahead. Perhaps there *was* something to live for once again. And perhaps just *living* mightn't be so difficult after all.

The hot August light was almost as sharp as that of an Australian summer. And the heat, the scraps of paper floating on odd gusts of wind in the empty square, the stacked restaurant chairs, the discarded soccer balls, the weeds in the cracks of the stones, the shuttered windows and closed doors gave everything a small-town vacancy.

Many of the people she knew were gone for the month, though luckily not Marco. Only a few from the school were still in town. The canals were low, like drained mudpools, and the city was too hot and fetid to be bothered with. Lucy was the only one in the popular residential square, and stood looking about it, deciding whether to keep walking or go back to the flat. She'd been practising all morning, had walked all afternoon, and now found herself in the more working-class area of Cannaregio.

Wind made her irritable. She'd gone out without thinking and the light summer dress she wore had been blown about. Men stared at her from the outside tables and through the windows of bars and cafés and restaurants in the squares, but she walked on, staring directly ahead as if none of them existed. And soon they didn't. Nothing mattered, because Lucy was leaving. She had decided this some time during the day. It was impulsive, sudden, impetuous perhaps, but certainly final. She couldn't stay. It was impossible.

By evening the wind had finally brought with it the tumbling clouds of cooler weather. She wasn't sure where she was going to escape to or what on earth she would do when she got there. She knew she needed a city, and memories of Paris, those times spent there with her parents (for which, at this very moment, she ached as she would never have thought she could), returned to her. At the small kitchen window that overlooked the canal she stared blankly ahead. In between the buildings she could just see through to another canal and another small bridge. And as she stood staring from the window, Lucy saw somebody she knew from the Conservatorium cross the bridge. What other

European city could be this intimate? she thought. But was it intimate? Or just plain small?

It seemed, after all, that Venice was a town, not a city, and she needed a city in which to lose herself, melt into the crowd. She allowed herself a half-smile, for she had always imagined herself above the crowd, destined to be one of the elect, but now she just wanted to disappear into it. She wanted to become anonymous, just anybody. And it seemed to her, as she stood looking through the window of what she now saw as her poky little flat, that she couldn't get out fast enough. Besides, she would do no one any good by staying—not Fortuny, not Marco, not herself.

She hadn't yet changed out of the dress she'd worn all day, and she recalled the men in the cafés, leaning forward in the dead of the afternoon to stare as the wind had blown her skirt about. She heard their whistles—and she heard Molly's long-ago voice telling her that only a tart walked like that. Only a tart in the wind could drag men's heads out of café windows. And maybe that's all she was, a tart that dragged men's heads out of café windows, the kind of tart that took old men for a ride. Now, and not for the first time in the last twenty-four hours, she wished she'd never come, had just let the thing be. Wished she'd just left Fortuny in the realm of daydream playthings, to be taken out and put aside at will. Nobody's heart broken, no one to carry the heavy burden of having broken it.

She saw that she'd left a paperback dictionary of art and artists lying on the table. Earlier that morning she'd been flicking through it when she'd come across an entry on Munch. After reading it, she had idly taken in the birth and death dates: 1863–1944. Odd, she had thought. But why odd? Then she remembered what Fortuny had told her about Munch, and how he had met the artist just after the war. She shrugged her shoulders, shook her head slowly. It was such a little thing, she thought, such a trivial fabrication. Why did he bother?

But it was too hot to think and too late to care. She washed the dust of the day off under the shower, changed into a pair of clean jeans and T-shirt, then wandered out into the tourist-cluttered night to meet Fortuny for the last time.

Chapter Thirteen

LUCY was relieved that Fortuny made no move to touch her when she arrived; neither did they sit on the couch in the salon. He ushered her up the stairs to the private living quarters of the house, where she had only been once before, and onto the balcony that faced the Grand Canal.

There, Rosa had set a table with wine and wafers, but this time the wine was a bottle of fine-quality champagne. As on all Lucy's previous visits, the lights of the square opposite, the traghetto stop and the cafés were reflected in the water. It had turned cool now, and they talked quietly as the sound of little wavelets in the canal lightly lapped against the foundations of the building.

Fortuny was always considerate, but this evening he was especially so. At one point Lucy shivered and he said, concern obvious in his voice, 'You are cold.'

She laughed. 'No.'

'Your shawl…' He was about to call for Rosa but Lucy stopped him.

'Please.'

'Shall we go in?' he asked.

'I'm not cold,' she said, a hint of irritation in her voice. 'And it's lovely looking over the canal.'

Fortuny relented, but continued to be attentive to the smallest details: the taste of the wafers; the suitability of the wine. And at the slightest hint of a breeze he rose from his chair and insisted on shifting. But Lucy remained unmoved and he sat down again.

It was mid-August and already the summer was almost over. But, Lucy knew, something more than summer was gone. The sparkle was gone from the waters, the music gone from the canals. And so, too, it was with Fortuny. Fortuny, and that old, old world he lived in. No longer charming, but weary of itself. It occurred to her then that the whole notion of tradition, of history, might even be a dreadful burden, passed with enormous relief from one generation to the next, gathering in weight and decreasing in meaning as the generations passed.

While she contemplated these thoughts, she also dwelt on that now distant Lucy who had dreamt herself into this world, the Lucy who had somehow imagined that this was her world too. Whatever had she been thinking? And who *was* that girl? But as much as she now tried to re-enter the mind of her earlier self, she couldn't. She was on the outside, looking in. The feeling unsettled her and, for the first time in memory, possibly the first time in her life, she saw herself as she could imagine others might. And she didn't much like what she saw. Not much at all, really. The eyes of Molly, the eyes of the Methodist Ladies College and of the Conservatorium were her eyes now. But it was, above all, through Marco's eyes that she now saw herself—foolish, headstrong, a scatterbrain even, who'd meddled with people's lives as if it were all a fabulous game, and who'd got herself in way over her head. She looked at Fortuny and now felt only guilt and compassion where she had once felt worship; felt sadness where there had once been a dreadful impatience to start the real living.

When the champagne was drunk, Fortuny led her back into the house and escorted her to the main dining room. Lucy had never seen the room before, didn't even know it existed. The house was deceptive in its vastness, a constant source of surprise. Knowing this house, she suddenly thought, was like knowing this whole intricate world into which she had stumbled, then suddenly not knowing it; being constantly called upon to adjust your perceptions of something you felt sure you had understood.

She had not expected to be dining in such surroundings and was conscious of her casual clothes, of having made no effort with her appearance. Fortuny, on the other hand—and she had noted this from the moment she had stepped into the house—gave every impression of having spent the afternoon grooming himself for the occasion. He was positively glowing, looking years younger than at any time since she had met him.

When dinner was over, the wines barely touched and the summer fruits, so painstakingly selected, all but ignored, Fortuny invited Lucy into an adjoining room. It was darker, but the low lamplight nevertheless revealed yet more portraits. They were hung all around the room and dated from around the late fifteenth century through to a portrait of a man and a woman dressed in the fashion of the early 1940s. Spread out on a large walnut table was a family tree, decorated in the style of an illuminated, medieval manuscript.

Fortuny was happy, his mood light, his manner and gestures those of a man of the world. But underneath it all, in the occasional, impatient brushing of his silvery hair back from his forehead, was a hint of anxiety. He leaned over the table, engrossed in the grand narrative spread out in front of him, discoursing on various names on the diagram, supplying their histories, describing them, momentarily bringing them back to life. But as much as Lucy was drawn to the tale, even absorbed in it, she once again found herself wondering what she was *doing* there, when Fortuny asked, 'How old is your family?'

Lucy, who was only vaguely aware of her mixed

English, Scottish and German stock, shrugged her shoulders.

'I'm really not sure.'

Her reply was not without a hint of defiance, as if to suggest that the past, illustrious or not, was not as important to her as it was to him.

'Well, I am,' Fortuny continued, sipping from a small glass of his Calvados. Sipping, Lucy thought, suddenly impatient with the whole scene. Always sipping. If only he would just gulp the stuff for once. 'In my family,' he said, lowering the glass, 'it is impossible to remain unaware of your history.'

'That must be very difficult.'

'Sometimes.' He nodded. 'At other times I feel the privilege, and when I say that I mean the honour. And there are times,' he added in a manner that Lucy thought a little too ponderous, 'I feel the burden.'

She nodded, not knowing what else to say.

'Will you sit down?'

'No, I'm quite happy standing.'

'Please. Please, sit down,' Fortuny said, and indicated a large padded armchair covered in rich swirling patterns. He guided her towards it.

'There!' He smiled, stepping back and admiring the scene with, it seemed to Lucy, the same delight he had shown when he had draped her in the red dress, or when he had arranged her at the window in the spring— those times that now seemed so impossibly distant. He broke into her thoughts, his voice rising with satisfaction. 'I can't believe that you have never sat in that chair before.'

'You make it sound like a throne.'

'My dear Lucia…'

'I'm not Lucia,' Lucy said, calm but definite.

Fortuny paused. 'My dear…Lucy. You make it look like a throne.'

He was smiling. Lucy looked about her then, briefly, returned the smile, deciding that the best thing to do was to play along. It couldn't do any harm.

'I think,' she said, quietly joking, 'that I could almost like being a matriarch.'

Fortuny, who was standing by the marble fireplace, cleared his throat and turned directly towards her.

'You are a very beautiful woman.'

Lucy inclined her head almost regally, nodding slightly.

'It was not a compliment,' he said with a slight raising of the eyebrow, his manner that of a man who has known and mixed with beautiful women all his life. 'It was simply a statement. Truthful. I've watched you,' he added. 'You have natural poise, a natural grace. It's in your blood. And, believe me, other people notice too. I've seen them look at you. You make people aware of your presence without trying, and that is a gift. Not many people have it. But you, dear Lucy, you have it.'

He gazed at her intently, looking her up and down much as one might study a portrait painting.

'Do you like this house?' he suddenly asked.

It was an odd question and Lucy, who had stopped playing along, was becoming increasingly uneasy.

'Of course I do. Why do you ask?'

'Some people don't.' Fortuny's voice was almost inaudible. 'Some people don't like it at all.'

'Oh.'

'They find it…' He paused again. 'How shall I put it? They find it oppressive.'

'Oppressive?'

'Yes. All the portraits, all the history. Constantly present.' He then looked at her directly, his voice rising slightly. 'But you don't?'

'No,' she added, warily.

'Do you imagine it to be the type of house that somebody could live in?'

'Yes.'

'Not a museum?'

'No.'

'Do you find it a living house?' he repeated, his voice rising, determined that the point be established.

'Yes,' Lucy said again, her tone now suggesting concern. 'Yes. A living house. That's a very nice way of putting it.' She was now shifting in the armchair. 'You live here. Your family breathes here.'

'But is that enough, dear Lucy?' Fortuny said, almost abstracted.

'I don't know. It seems like a lot to me.'

'But not to me.' He ran his fingers through his hair again, adjusted the handkerchief in his breast pocket and leaned back against the fireplace, his palms resting against the cool stone. 'You, my dear Lucy. Would you like to live in this house?'

Lucy suddenly stopped shifting in her seat.

'Here?'

'Yes.'

'I don't understand.' But she did understand, and wished desperately that there was some way she could stop him from speaking the words he was surely about to utter. 'I have a place,' she said.

Fortuny pushed his palms against the marble and looked at the ceiling for a moment. Lucy was perfectly still in her chair. Don't, she thought. Don't, Signor Fortuny. But he did, and she looked away as his voice returned.

'It's very simple.' He closed his eyes a moment, then opened them and went on. 'My dear, dear Lucy. I would be deeply honoured if you would consent to be my wife.'

His formality, his manner of address, his speech, his actions, the delicacy of his hand movements in guiding her to a chair or to another room. The fact that he had made no sexual advances to her recently, had not attempted to touch her as before, had required nothing of her. That he had adopted the manner of a suitor, concerned for her every whim… All of this now fell sadly, absurdly into place. He had been *courting* her.

'I am no longer quite the young man I once was. This I know.' (Said, Lucy couldn't help but observe, with the false modesty of a man famous for having been barely touched by the years.) 'But I would be deeply honoured, my dear, dear Lucy.'

Fortuny now stood in the centre of the room, portraits of preceding generations all around him, his hands by his sides.

'Lucy?'

The vast house was silent. Not even the echoes of the canal, the boats on the water or the slapping sound of their wake pierced the quiet. Nothing. Only the softly whispered sound of her name in the air, the question still unanswered. She closed her eyes, remained motionless for a moment, then shook her head.

Fortuny stepped closer, his legs slightly apart on the rug, his head bowed a little and his forefinger tracing the lines of his brow.

'Dear Lucy, you say no and the house dies.' He then paused, emphasising the silence of the room. 'Do you hear that?'

But Lucy shook her head again, forced herself to speak. 'It's impossible, Paolo. My dear, dear Paolo. It is an impossible request. I have no intention of marrying you or anybody. I should never have come here. I should never have imposed.' She looked about the room, searching for the right words, a girl, just a girl, with someone's heart in her hands. 'Besides, I'm leaving.'

'L-leaving?' he stammered, running his fingers nervously through his hair and taking on a dishevelled look. 'Leaving?' he repeated, as if it were an impossibility.

'Yes.'

'But I welcomed you into my world.'

'Yes.'

'Do you not have the slightest idea how hard it is to enter this world?'

'Oh, dear Paolo, I do, I do.' But her voice wavered as she spoke, knowing full well she could never explain just how much she understood.

'And now,' Fortuny went on, 'now I offer you that world.'

'But it is not *my* world, Paolo,' she said, her distress evident. 'I could never live in it.'

He stood still, nowhere left to go. Then he spoke, a vague look of incomprehension across his features and not really addressing her directly. 'I taught you. Me. Fortuny!'

Then he stepped, physically imposing, closer to Lucy's armchair, his body seeming to have somehow expanded with passion. He was almost transformed, some other Fortuny, one who Marco had warned her about and whom she'd caught hints of before. And, not for the first time, Lucy was even a little frightened of him.

'Dear Lucy. I gave you my secrets. All my little ways.'

'I know,' Lucy said. 'And I thank you. Believe me, Signor Fortuny, I thank you.'

'You thank me?' he repeated, nodding to himself, his voice rising this time in open anger. 'You *thank* me?'

'Yes. And so much more that I can't begin to explain.' She was almost pleading with him to understand.

'I taught you. I taught you *everything*.' And he looked her up and down as if to suggest that it was more than music he had in mind, that he had taken the raw material that had been Lucy and had worked wonders; that the Lucy who stood before him now was the fruit of his labour, the creation of Fortuny himself. 'Is it not in you to thank me a little more?'

She shook her head, her eyes imploring.

'But, my dear girl,' Fortuny said, lowering his voice again, 'you have not considered my proposal. You answer without thinking. And,' he added, with a sweeping gesture that seemed to encompass the portraits, the room, the house itself, 'it is a proposal that deserves to be considered.'

'And I have considered it.'

'But I would give you *everything*!'

His voice was suddenly shrill in the air, offending the quiet dignity of the room, and he stopped for a moment as if distantly registering that the evening was not progressing as he had profoundly hoped. But his pause was only momentary; he then fell to his knees on the rug, gripped her wrists, threw his head back towards the ceiling where circles of light from the lamps overlapped like so many moons in a crowded sky, then whispered her name again as he rocked back and forth.

'My dearest Lucia—'

'Don't call me that.'

'I would be deeply, deeply—"

'No!'

The grip of his hands was once again strong and it was only as she rose from the armchair that she managed to shake herself free. She turned in the doorway.

'I can't stay any longer, Paolo. I have already stayed too long. I have done too much.'

He looked at her as if to speak again, but said nothing. Lucy continued, her lips trembling. 'I hope, dear Paolo, oh, I so hope that our time together has given you pleasure. The pleasure that it has given me, the pleasure that you have always given me. But I cannot do what you ask, I just can't.' She felt the pricking of tears and quickly wiped her eyes. 'Believe me, Paolo, you will always be with me. Wherever I go, whatever I do. You will always be there… No,' she added, as he stood up. 'Don't see me out. Please. I'll find my way.'

She rushed from the room, unaware that she had left her shawl which had dropped behind a chair, and passed Rosa, who was standing in the hallway. She ran towards the salon door that led down into the court-yard, but before she reached the door a thin, sinewy hand gripped her shoulder. She turned, fully expecting to be confronted by Fortuny, but found Rosa instead.

'*Schee!*'

Rosa spat the word into the face of this young foreign woman, who was always going to be trouble, and at first Lucy couldn't understand. But she understood everything as Rosa repeated herself and slapped the palm of her hand hard into the crotch of Lucy's jeans as she spoke.

'*Schee!*'

Lucy spun round on the marble floor of the salon and groped for the door while Rosa spat the old Venetian word once more into her face.

As she ran from the house, Fortuny's deep, almost guttural voice, and the strangest, the most beautifully incomprehensible words, seemed to hang in the air. Say no, his voice said, and the house dies. Say yes, and it lives. The house, the history, the thousand-year tradition it shelters. With Lucy (and here she shook her head again and again) not only the receptacle of the family seed but the eventual inheritor of the entire history, the mere contemplated dead weight of which she seemed to be shrugging off as she shivered in the cool air. A receptacle as sacred as the sacred tradition she would carry within her, then pass on so that everything might continue, rolling through her life with the inexorability of an empire, eventually absorbing her into the timeless world of the house. The dream was no longer hers and the most enchanting of myths had ceased to enchant. No. No more.

When she reached the Accademia bridge, she stood still for a moment, taking deep breaths of the moist air, almost gasping, until the natural rhythms of her body began to settle and she crossed over to the square on the other side. 'I will,' she muttered to the dark lanes around her, 'I *will* find my way.'

In the library, Fortuny ran Lucy's shawl through his fingers, noting how smoothly the silk passed through them, like sand on a beach or time enclosed in glass.

When Rosa opened the door moments later the room was in semi-darkness and she could only just make out the table, champagne still in the glasses. She saw Fortuny, now kneeling in front of the large armchair where Lucy had sat, as if kneeling before invisible royalty to receive the sword of knighthood or the sentence of death. As she slowly pushed the door further and the hallway light entered the room, his head suddenly jerked up.

'Go to hell.'

His hair had fallen over his face, but his eyes stared back at her, wide like a drunk's. He resumed his supplicating pose, and Rosa quickly shut the door.

Fortuny was slumped in the salon. He had been there for more than three hours, in the same chair, in front of the same painting, unmoving. Rosa had long since been dismissed for the evening, and the house was as still and as silent as the many scenes that hung from its walls. He had carried Lucy's shawl from the library, holding it in his hands as he stared into the painting, stroking the smooth, silky material with his fingers and breathing in the faint scent of her perfume.

Then, for a moment, his eyes shifted to the large painting facing the couch, a portrait of a woman dressed in the style of the 1940s. Elena, the woman depicted, had been Fortuny's first lover. She had been forty-one, the lonely wife of an indifferent bureaucrat; he had been nineteen. The painting, completed in the first few weeks of the affair, had been a gift from a friend who, Fortuny reflected, had never amounted to anything much.

Elena... Once the salon had been filled with her name, when the young Fortuny, free of parental constraints, had entered the world of adult love. But the affair had quickly become tiresome and only lasted a matter of months. He recalled how Elena had hung upon him at engagements; how she had hung upon his every word, his every phrase, telephoned him at odd times of the day, and endured his dismissiveness.

But what he remembered most were their final engagements, their final days: interminable afternoons at her house, which he could hardly wait to leave. He recollected the long silences between them, broken by Elena's voice, going on and on about his youth, telling him how lucky he was. How he didn't know what he possessed because youth never does. And how, she knew perfectly well, he would one day leave her on just such an afternoon as this.

She came to mind, Fortuny reflected, only because he'd recently found references to her in his father's diaries. References, he concluded, which suggested that their relations, too, had been more than friendly; suggested to Fortuny, for the first time, the possibility that poor Elena had suffered the indignity of being jilted by both father and son.

But that, he quietly marvelled to himself, was almost forty years ago. Now this room, this house, would be forever filled with Lucy, and it was Fortuny who was left with only the last, hastily departing footsteps of youth to recall and dwell upon. Fortuny, with only those uncluttered, endless hours of age in which to recall again and again how his resurrection had slipped from him. How hope had gone when Lucy had fled from the house. Lucy, now chasing life.

Before she had arrived the past had at least been a completed act. Now everything would be Lucy, a constant reminder of what had almost come to pass. Where she'd sat, the cello that would never be played again but whose music was still audible in his head; the window, the chairs, the wineglasses, the vine in the courtyard against which she had once brushed but would never pass again.

Only her remembered presence was left. And her scarf, as if dropped on the floor precisely at that moment before the corporeal being stepped into the region of consoling myth. *And the hair that fell to her thighs.* This fabulous creature, who called from the sea, had now returned to the sea. Now, there on the wall in front of him, only to be gazed upon, the most enchanting of myths. And the scarf the last vestige of what really was.

Lucy soon left the square behind her. She couldn't face the silence of her flat so, as she crossed the Accademia bridge, her steps took her towards the café where the few students of the Conservatorium still left in the town played, simply for their own pleasure.

As she passed below the Rialto, looking up at the line of its white marble steps in the night, it seemed to Lucy that she would always carry the image of Fortuny standing in front of her, tie askew, hair tossed forward across his forehead, pleading for the impossible.

Her hands were still trembling as she paused for a moment on a small bridge, running her fingers over its wrought-iron work. Two men passed, smoking and talking, but momentarily puzzled by her. When they were gone and the bridge was deserted again, she gripped the railings as if there were nothing else in the world left for her to hang on to, and hang on to something she must, for that was her immediate task.

And it was then that she heard it: a groan, the soft howl of a wounded animal. At first it seemed to come from beside or behind her, and she looked about for the source of the sound. But, of course, there was no one and nothing there. *She* was the sound, this sound that welled up inside her and poured forth as it was always going to, for someone's heart was always going to break—only she had never thought it would be hers.

And it was here, her eyes closed as she hugged the metal railing of the bridge, that she heard the music that had roused her all those years ago. It came from the windows, the doorways and alleyways all around her, faint at first but unmistakeable, then gradually louder—louder until every cobblestone and building, and every nerve in her own shaking body, reverberated to the saddest of music. For a moment she was once again the Lucy who had wished herself into Fortuny's world, but the groan of anguish that she barely recognised as hers continued to pour from her in deep, violent breaths like sobs, until she heard and felt nothing…

When Lucy came to, she realised she was slumped on the bridge, leaning her head against the railings, with no memory of how she had got into that position and no sense of just how long she had been there. Her breathing was steady now and the animal groan had left her, but she was utterly spent and had no strength left to get up off the ground, let alone walk away. She ran her fingers over the square stones of the footpath, almost mesmerised, wondering how on earth she came to be sitting on it. When she at last looked around her, she was confronted with the spectacle of the silver streetlights, the cool, neat lines of the tiny canal, and the clean, sharp edges of buildings seeming somehow insubstantial, like a cardboard stage glowing under the artificial lights. This was, after all, a place where dreams just might fall out of the sky, mingling with the everyday while they set about the sad and dreary business of coming true. Lucy suddenly felt old. Old beyond her years, as though she would never feel young again.

At last she lifted herself up, steadied her legs, and stepped off the bridge. She followed the curve of the walkway that eventually led to the railway station and, just for a moment, saw herself as she was when she had first arrived in the clear, chilly weather of early March. Saw herself sitting on the station steps, her bags at her feet, her cello by her side, waiting for everything—for life—to begin. And she ached to take back the past, to recover the dream unlived: to have that perpetual possibility, that world of speculation to which she could always go and which would always be there for her, to be taken out, toyed with, and put aside at will.

Most of Cannaregio was closed up for the night, but not the café, the aptly named Paradise Lost, where Lucy stood at the front window, looking in and listening to the music. She could see the faces of friends from the Conservatorium, who sat in a group at the café's one large table, quietly talking or just listening to the music. Vaguely envious, she gazed at her friends for a moment, at the light playing on their wineglasses, at the curling blue smoke of their cigarettes and the animation of their laughter, soundless from where she stood.

She had come to see Marco, if only for one last time, but he wasn't there. So it should be, she thought. So it should be. What was there to say, anyway? That he was right? That she *had* gone in over her head? No, there was too much to say, and it was too late to say it. And what would it accomplish other than to drag somebody else into her mess? So, he wasn't there and it was for the best. No need to linger. As she turned from the café she caught sight of herself in the window, but—could that really be her? She looked again and saw her smeared eyes, saw how her make-up had run, saw her hair unkempt, as if she'd just woken. But it was the eyes that drew her in: tired eyes ringed with dark circles of fatigue, far too tired for her years. But it was her all right that she was looking at, and once again she felt old, felt she could never be young again. Suddenly the word haggard came to her, for it was a haggard figure standing before her. She turned away in shock and despair and quickly fled from her reflection.

The clear edges of the buildings, solid and silent, were defined by the lights along the canal. There were no voices to be heard, no laughter in the dark, nobody watching over the scene. No invisible hands were guiding our destinies, Lucy thought. No gods, or dark commanding figures, half gods, half men, surveying all beneath them with the all-seeing eyes of the elect. Just us, she thought as she stumbled through the dark corners and night-lit streets of the city. Nobody else. Just us.

She left quietly the next morning, early enough to avoid seeing anybody. She left with an overnight bag and her cello. The rest she would send for. And when she passed the post box, she dropped a single letter in, addressed to Marco. She'd come to see him at the café, she'd written, and he wasn't there. Lucky Marco, she'd added, lucky you, Lucy wasn't much fun at the moment. And, sad to say, she'd gone on, there'd be no more cha-cha, and the baby elephants would have to walk without her.

PART FIVE

Chapter Fourteen

OVER the following weeks Fortuny was seen wandering the streets and lanes of the city, searching in café windows, squares, bookstores and passing water buses for a glimpse of Lucy. He searched in the gardens of Castello, the Schiavoni at sunset and Cannaregio after nightfall, alert for the flow of her hair, her long strides, her laughter and her eyes of the deepest green.

Sometimes he was almost satisfied by the memory of a place—a statue, perhaps, that she may have paused at or leaned against during their social outings. Once he stopped at a fountain in San Marco near the Fenice. There, he relived the night, the splash, as Lucy had cooled her face and shaken the water from her. The memory even brought a measure of temporary comfort.

But once at home the torment of the nights would begin. He had called Lucy's number but it had been disconnected; nobody answered when he knocked at the door of her flat. And so, during those weeks, he sat in his study night after night, unable to sleep, unable even to sit before the soothing scene of the *Birth of Venus*. And outside, where lately the water taxis had played like dolphins, was only the monotonous thrum of the city's traffic.

Then, one morning, somebody at the Conservatorium casually mentioned that Lucy had left, been gone for weeks. Fortuny stopped his walks and retired within the walls of his house, with its paintings and its library. The days shortened and autumn cooled into winter. Gradually, in the dark blue nights of that winter, the dream of Lucy began to dim and, as it faded, so did Fortuny's faith, his strength of will, until he no longer had the heart to keep it alive.

One evening, sitting in his salon, he leaned his tired head back in his armchair and felt his body slipping into the irresistible lassitude of defeat. And, in spite of a voice saying don't—don't give those feelings away, for this is where the girl dies—Fortuny relaxed. He knew that his claims on the heart of his Lucia were forever lost to him and, as he gave it all up, the pain began to ease. And when his fingers and hands relinquished their grip on the arms of the chair and he expelled the air in his lungs, it was with a deep, sighing breath like the dying fall of exhausted music, its phrases, finally, all played out.

Months later, in one of the seven rooms of Florian's Café, Fortuny was entertaining over a dozen guests from the Conservatorium, instructors and students, gathered to mark the departure of a young man named Marco Mazetti, a nimble young violinist familiar to Fortuny from visits to the school and because he had seen him performing with Lucy in the square. Big things were expected of this Mazetti, who was leaving for Rome, and Fortuny, in a jovial mood, felt unexpected sympathy for him, having himself left the city for Rome as a young man.

The lights were low in the room and cast shadows across the bright, gold ceiling, causing its rococo patterns to swirl in and out of light and dark. The portraits on the cluttered walls periodically reflected the shadow play of the guests. Some sitting down, others standing at the tables of the room, their heads, now inclined in concentrated attention, now thrown back in laughter. Outside, the vast drawing room that was the Piazza San Marco was draped in blue winter light and closed for the season.

Inside, Fortuny was entertaining the company at his table with stories of his performances, his concert tours, his travels. Carla, once more his occasional companion at social events, sat at the same table, listening. He was enjoying himself, talking more freely than he'd talked for some time and, Carla noticed, drinking more. A lot more. Perhaps she ought to tell him but, observing how he was clearly relishing the company, she decided to let it be.

Among Fortuny's stories was the tale of an extended stay in London in the early 1960s, when he had recorded the Bach Suites at the Abbey Road studios. During one of the sessions, a young, long-haired pop musician had watched intently from the production desk and had approached him in the break to compliment him on his playing. Fortuny laughed, and broke into slurred English. 'That was gear.' He paused a moment, then asked his young audience, 'What was this *gear* that he told me?' It was, he added, his only meeting with one of the Beatles, even though they had both continued to record in the same studios for most of the decade. And, furthermore, he never knew which Beatle it was. 'They all looked the same to me.' He laughed, throwing down the last of his brandy and immediately ordering more.

He moved on to stories about Ireland, Spain and the unmentionable west coast of America. He held the table in thrall, all of them leaning forward as if afraid they might miss something—all except Marco, who watched the Maestro with amused detachment. Outside, light rain began falling and Carla rose, kissed Fortuny on the cheek, and quietly excused herself, pointing to her watch and remarking on the darkness and rain. Fortuny waved, then turned back to the table, the talk continuing and the wine and brandy flowing.

Waiters disappeared, to materialise again into the

soft light with silver trays of petits fours, with drinks, with savouries. It suited them all, this café society, with its pastiche of languages and accents that could be identified at close range but was a babble from the fringes. Here was a painted scene, gradually dying in the tar base of its own pigments, the efforts of everybody—the master, the models, the carefully constructed poses and the restorers—all doomed to darkness. But for the moment they sat in the café's light and shade, where Fortuny's resonant voice, an occasional slur betraying the amount he had drunk, held the attention of his guests.

'I can only say one knows these things,' Fortuny said, his tone now more reflective as he talked of retirement, the timing of it all, of recognising the moment.

'It's a matter of knowing when something is over. We can't teach these things, one simply knows, or one doesn't. But leaving it all,' he concluded, a faint smile on his lips, 'should be like leaving a love affair in the full summer of its passion, that moment when its ripeness is absolute, before the first shadow falls.' He closed his eyes a moment, then looked about the table. 'Ripeness is all, eh?' Then he smiled.

But the table around him was silent, and he didn't notice two students who glanced knowingly at each other and raised their eyebrows. It was then that Fortuny turned to toast Marco, a salute, he said, to the future, to success and to life. Marco, at the end of the table, raised his glass and returned the toast as the whole table joined in.

Soon after, the company rose as one. As they took their leave and dispersed into the night, Fortuny, now noticeably unsteady on his feet, waved to Marco, called out something, but the words remained inaudible, drowned out by the weather.

Rain was falling steadily on the square. Fortuny walked slowly along the Procuratie Nuove, his hands dangling in his pockets, his head tilted. He stepped from the cover of the square into the web of lanes that ran off it. A couple under an umbrella ran towards the colonnade, quickly glancing at the man standing completely still in the rain, apparently deep in thought as though trying to recall a matter of great importance. With his shoulders fallen into a stoop he stood, a still, dark figure in a Homburg hat, liquefying in the rain.

Then the sky opened and the now heavy rain bucketed down. Noticing that the metal gate of a *sotoportego* had been left ajar, Fortuny slipped into the dark, covered passageway and followed it, constantly going over the conversation in the café, tossed between happy remembrance and the nagging thought that he might have overdone things, laid it on a bit thick and talked just a little too much. There were no lights inside the *sotoportego* and he could have been in the subterranean vaults of an old palace. He stumbled in the dark, rested his hand against the wall, then continued towards the dull, grey light at the end of the passageway. Still absorbed in his fragmented recollections of the evening and barely aware that the excessive quantity of brandy was taking effect, he came out into the street again and back into the rain.

With his drenched hat wilting over his eyes, Fortuny hurried along the small calle that ran off the *sotoportego*, and in a matter of seconds found himself standing at the main thoroughfare of the Frezzeria. It was then that Fortuny, native of the city, lifetime resident of Dorsoduro, the evening's brandy coursing through his veins, swayed from side to side where he stood and, instead of turning left and thereby making his way home, mistakenly turned right. Head down, he strode forward with the confident abandon of the lifetime resident, assuming his feet would always point him in the right direction and the compass of his instincts take him home.

Still thinking about the evening, he suddenly remembered the furtive, knowing looks exchanged between some of the students, suggesting that the Maestro might have had a bit too much... Fortuny, without even bothering to look, lurched into another *sotoportego* to escape the incessant rain. Here, in the low, dark passageway, with cobwebs all around, electrical wires hanging from the walls, and the acrid stench of urine whipped up by the wind and rain, he came to an unfamiliar boat landing and stood still.

Then something remarkable happened, something that had never happened before. Fortuny paused, peered about him, squinting out into the night, and realised with a sudden shock that he was lost. It was impossible, but the more he looked around, the less familiar everything became. No cafés, no shops, no names to mark his position. Even the buildings along the canal, indistinct in the rain, were indistinguishable from one another. Beside him, the canal was clearly rising, and the rain, like wave after wave of formation bombing, pockmarked the surface of the water. Surely he was walking in the right direction? It *had* to be the way home. But the rain, now falling in sheets, and the brandy pumping through his veins suddenly made everything impossible. Confused, absurdly helpless, he turned this way and that in the passageway, the stones smooth and slippery under his feet and not a soul to ask.

It was then, on the grey waters of the rising canal, that the slow, smooth bow of a gondola passed across the opening where the passageway ended. Empty, its gold embellishments shining in the rain, the boat floated silently by in black majesty. It had come loose from its moorings and found its way into the canals, carried by the currents. Fortuny watched the gondola pass, silent and tantalising. His coat, wrapped about him like a cape, was leaden with the rain, and he wavered on the spot, staring down into the canal, which was now swelling and rising to meet the edges of the landing steps.

Still standing on those steps and peering through the downpour, Fortuny eyed the small bridge in front of him. He detected a sign attached to the corner of a building opposite, possibly a street name, but the rendering had fallen away and he couldn't read it. It was then that he leaned forward, trying to get closer, to read the name of the bridge through the iron grille work. But the name still eluded him and, with his hands on the wall of the *sotoportego*, he leaned even further forward so as to see better. Then, in his effort, he slipped on the grey moss of the steps, his feet gave way under the smooth, worn stones, and Fortuny fell.

Somebody's sleep may have been vaguely disturbed, but it was an incidental and unremarkable enough sound to pass unnoticed. A splash, a brief flurry of arms and legs flaying the water like the tiny legs of a beetle, trying to regain its feet. But Fortuny had fallen face down, his sodden coat weighing upon him like chain metal, and the more he splashed in the swollen canal, the more exhausted he became. His head was below the water and the viscous lime green of the canal was already beginning to enter his lungs, although he was still conscious that the stone steps, the edge of the canal itself, was just out there. If only he could lift his body he could grasp that edge and dredge himself from a canal he would have crossed regularly, without even noticing it, all his life. But that edge was just beyond his reach…

Then, miraculously, he was able to lift his head for a moment or two, and caught a glimpse of a vaguely familiar scene through the odd angles of his vision. Somewhere he heard voices, people calling to each other, and he saw the canal mailbox marked Ivo's, the name of a familiar restaurant at which he had often dined. Ivo's. Suddenly, Fortuny knew exactly where he was, knew that his house was no further than a ten-minute stroll away. And the thought of simply rising and taking that stroll home, the ease of it all, passed through his mind before his face dropped back into the canal.

Rubbish floated around him. Plastic wrappers, cigarette butts, chunks of bread. Soon the thrashing of Fortuny's arms and legs slowed, his mind became dull, and he seemed to be drifting into the most inviting, the most delightful of sleeps. As the canal oozed into him and the rain clawed at his back, Fortuny's arms and legs stopped moving altogether, the thunder of the rain in his ears fell silent, and he began slowly drifting with the flow of the canal, almost like a bather at peace on the calm waters of a summer beach.

And it was at this point, with one last gigantic effort

(remembering that he was, after all, still alive, and not about to snuff it just yet, thank you very much!) that he managed to heave himself round, his drunken, delirious eyes vaguely taking in the dark, liquid sky and the buildings about him, his head, his nose now just above the water line, now below it. With no strength left in him to do anything but drift, his mind floated in and out of consciousness, the world a dream. Fortuny's hat, which had tipped from his head as he'd fallen, now floated ahead of him along the surface of the canal, leaving his silver hair to swim about his skull like a wreath.

In this way, along the swollen canals and under the heavy rain that would surely bring with it the *aqua alta* in the morning, Paolo Fortuny, the Maestro, scion of a distinguished lineage, began his last tour of the city.

Fortuny didn't know it, or perhaps he did in those last seconds of consciousness, but he had fallen into a small canal in San Marco—a small canal that flowed into the Rio di San Moise—past the Hotel Bauer Grunwald, and into the expanse of the Grand Canal, where rows of black gondolas would sit waiting for his arrival like so many black cabs.

With his hat preceding him, Fortuny moved through the dark, rainy city. First, along the Rio dei Barcarrolli. He floated by San Fantin, with the façade of the Fenice somewhere behind it, then passed his stationer's store, now dark, its metal awnings drawn for the night. Inside, the crisply printed envelopes, the etched writing paper, the prints of old Venice awaited the day's commerce. In a few hours, on a rainy Wednesday morning, the owner, whom Fortuny had known all his life, would open the door of L'Art D'Écrire, and trade, the lifeblood of the city, would continue as usual. But for the moment the shop was silent and empty, but for only the ghost image of its owner smiling in the doorway as he waved one last time to the passing figure of Don Fortuny, whose custom it had always been a privilege to receive.

Past the Calle Venier, filled with overflowing restaurant bins and the rubbish of tourism, and past the stained and jumbled façade of San Moise itself, Fortuny flowed out into the waters of the Grand Canal and came face to face with the shining domes of the Salute, which he had fully intended to visit again, if only for the Titians and Tintorettos in the sacristy. And then, as if his body were directing itself (but was, in fact, being directed by the tidal change), Fortuny moved left and turned back into the town along the canal. His hat, by now, had gone on ahead.

To his left was the Guggenheim museum and then the Accademia bridge, that wooden span over which he had strolled every day of his life, and near which, as a young man, he had witnessed the disappearing figure of Ezra Pound, with his hat, his stick, and his coat wrapped about him like a cape.

Then, a short walk beyond the bridge, just back from the canal, the crumbling Renaissance palace that housed the Conservatoire of Music. The building would be still and dark, but that joyous jumble of pianos, flutes, horns, drums and the lilting ache of cellos and strings floated over the water, through the rain, to the passing figure of the Maestro, with each of those young players no doubt anxiously looking up at the completion of their exercises for the Maestro's judgement: a slight nod, a smile perhaps, or an impassive stare. And somewhere the memory of one indissoluble morning when a young creature, with sun-coloured hair that fell to her side, appeared before him; appeared, spoke, and created a wave of exquisite pain beneath Fortuny's heart. No, not even a wave but a swell of the deepest green that would somewhere become a wave. And, in the rain, his heart heaved once more, reliving that moment of anticipated arrest, too exquisite to be endured...

And then, rolling in from the swollen basin, a dark wave washed up against him, bobbed him about, this way and that, and his head fell back below the waterline and stayed there, the canal now freely entering his lungs as he surrendered himself to that swell of the deepest green, the first intimations of which had been felt that now distant spring morning.

Floating under the bridge on the rising waters of the *aqua alta*, the motionless body of Fortuny now approached the Arabian arches, the *piano nobile*, of the vast house in which his family had lived for the past six hundred years. The lights were still on and Rosa, miserable with worry about the lateness of the hour and the absence of the master from the house, stared out into the grey rain, endlessly running her rosary through her fingers while the last of the family line passed by below.

Uncharacteristically, Rosa had telephoned the Conservatorium, then Florian's, to no avail. Later that morning, with a loyal and desperate heart, she would telephone the Questura and list Signor Paolo Fortuny as one of the missing persons of the city.

And so, through the grey hours of the early morning, the Grand Canal free of all traffic and impediments to progress, Fortuny journeyed through the sleeping heart of his city. Past canals casually bearing such names as Foscari; through San Polo, under the marble steps of the Rialto Bridge, Santa Croce, and on to the quieter houses of Cannaregio. And all the time the rain fell, steadily and heavily from a low, dark sky, the canals continued rising, and the first of the *aqua alta* spilled onto the low squares of Venice like the waters of the original swamp, temporarily reclaiming the city as they one day surely would forever.

* * *

As the early-morning council workers assembled the first of the ramparts over the many flooded squares of the city, majestically, almost regally, Fortuny was washed up against the edges of the Fondamenta Santa Lucia. A shopkeeper on his way to work was the first to notice the body and waved urgently to a police boat slowly cruising the canal. When the body was hauled from the water and slapped onto the steps of the station, the two policemen checked the papers, still inside the dark coat of Signor Fortuny, nodded to each other as a small crowd gathered in the rain, then telephoned the Questura from the launch.

During that morning and afternoon, slowly, softly, as the rain continued to fall, news that the Maestro had passed away in the night began to filter through the city. He had last been seen in a café in San Marco, and how his body, which had been dead eight hours, found its way to the Ferrovia Santa Lucia was a puzzle to everybody. The currents would surely run irresistibly back into the Basin of San Marco. But the tidal change took only a few hours, its wash flowed back into the city and in this rain, the policemen shrugged, who knew what could happen?

In Dorsoduro, a black Homburg was washed up onto the flooded Campo San Vio, where it remained wedged under a wooden rampart while the gumboots and galoshes, the feet of the city's workers, passed over it in the dull midweek light.

Epilogue

LUCY strolled across the bridge towards the boulevard St Michel. There was a sharp, clean wind and the promise of rain in the air. Soon it would be spring, then summer again. The boats on the river would be filled with tourists, the busy morning sun would lounge in the afternoons, and the café tables would continue to spill out onto the pavements in the evenings.

At one point she paused to lean over the railing and watch the Seine slowly flowing beneath her. Her glance then followed the river to where it divided in two and flowed round the old islands of the city, the embankments of the Ile de la Cité itself still in the waters like the bows of an anchored dreadnought. Suddenly a flat barge, laden with wooden crates, emerged from under the bridge and stirred the waters, its wake slapping the edges of the river and spilling onto the stone pavements where the dog owners walked by day and the vagrants slept by night. The week before this had been a tumid river, swollen by the rains; now, it had returned to a steady flow and the Paris fishermen were back.

Lucy had been living in Paris for over five months now, at first in a hotel room near the university, then in a small studio just back from the river, near the Pompidou. She hadn't written to Fortuny, had left no forwarding address in Venice, and, consequently, had received no forwarded mail, only a letter from Rona, a student from the Conservatorium who she had bumped into at a concert not long after she'd arrived in Paris. Rona had written to tell her, among other things, that Marco had received high praise from the newspaper critics in Rome. Marco, she went on, was on the road to fame, and everybody was so proud of him.

As she'd read the letter, she'd imagined him being photographed in some ill-tempered session one summer, and some girl thousands of miles away falling in love with a young Marco's moody, studio stare. She'd been on the point of mailing him that five-pound note, but had then hesitated. He would never remember their silly little bet, she thought, made what now seemed years rather than months ago, and she never posted it. But she kept the note in her purse long afterwards, waiting for the right moment yet knowing in her heart of hearts that she'd missed the moment in more ways than one. Besides, she told herself, he was on the road to being famous now, and didn't need old friends hanging on.

And Marco, after his well-publicised success, waited

for a letter containing a five-pound note, a letter that never came. After months had passed, he assumed that Lucy must never have seen the notices, but, as much as people told him he was destined for the top, he believed true fame would only ever come when a five-pound note arrived in the mail.

Normally, Lucy worked all through the morning, but because of the rare sunshine after the days of heavy rain that had been general across Europe the previous week she had decided to enjoy the late-winter sun with a newspaper.

At first the landmarks of the city, the cafés, the boulevards and bridges, even the leaves in the air and the river itself, had depressed her, but her mood had lifted lately. Now she sat turning the pages of her paper and, from time to time, glancing at the shops opposite and idly noting the shoots coming up on the branches of the plane trees. For a few moments she closed her eyes in the sunshine, envisioning the square and the café in the approaching spring and summer.

But when Lucy went back to her newspaper and turned the page, there was Fortuny. Yes, there was no mistake. It was Signor Paolo Fortuny, Il Maestro, his face artfully caught in half-shadow, his hair swept back, his eyes, shining, confident, assured.

Suddenly Lucy was thirteen again. That photograph

(now stored away with old exercise books and school texts in her old room at home) was all it took and she was swept back into childhood, carried by currents she was powerless to resist. She became, once more, the girl who played the cello every night in order to feel absolutely nothing. Those long summers, those warm, lonely nights when the idea of Fortuny's world first captured her, now returned, a part of her that could be shoved aside by time but never lost. The living of it, the intensity, the wish to have it all and yet to be free of it all, nostalgia and desire and the creeping emotions of the old dream... Lucy closed her eyes and the first shadow of the day fell across the sunlit square.

The obituary devoted most of its space to the musical achievements of the Venetian cellist who had retained his regional popularity but had fallen out of fashion with most European audiences and critics over the years. It touched lightly on the circumstances of his death, saying only that he had drowned the previous week, having apparently lost his footing, perhaps his way, during a night of heavy rain which had created flooding.

Lucy looked up, dazed, and stared unseeingly at the traffic across the bridge. Lost? Drowned? Odd. That wasn't her Fortuny. That miscellany of days and nights she'd spent in Venice, the jumble of memories, rose in her like the scraps and leaves of the street, uplifted by a sudden gust of wind, looking for a place settle.

Fortuny's house, those Arabian arches, the columns, the simple unadorned balcony of the *piano nobile*, which she would always remember as all milky grey in the moonlight, would die with Fortuny. Was already dead. No more footsteps on the marble floors, no music, no sound of that ancient language which had risen from some forgotten corner of history and spoke of oceans, fields and years. In the courtyard, there would perhaps be an early spring breeze drifting through the new shoots of jasmine, worrying, as it went, the old, creeping vines of wisteria. But no more movement or hint of life than that, for the garden, like the house, would be unoccupied. Signs of neglect, weeds flourishing in the hanging baskets and tangled vines, would soon be evident.

Inside, white sheets must now cover the furniture of the salon, the couch, the piano, the stool and Fortuny's armchair. Similarly, the study, the library, the dining room—and the bedroom. All the rooms of the house. And only those paintings of no monetary value would be left on the walls: those carefree figures wrapped in their post-war fashions, and the impeccable copy of the *Birth of Venus*. Airless rooms and the musty smell of a dead house, a house from which the private living has gone and a family's history has ended.

When Lucy shook herself free of her thoughts and looked back up at the day, it had clouded over and the wintry chill sent a shiver through her bones. She rose, folding the paper under her arm, and walked briskly back to her studio.

That wood, hard and yellowed with age, 'William Hills & Co., 1893', glowed in the corner of her room. Lucy hadn't played the cello all day, or the day before, or the day before that. Not for a week, in fact, since she'd read of Fortuny's death. She hadn't even picked it up, hadn't even tried. Now she sat in her cold studio flat, listening to the couple arguing upstairs while she vaguely registered the shape and colour of the instrument while allowing her mind to drift between the present and the past. One moment she would hear the Paris traffic outside her window; the next Fortuny's fingers closed on hers as he said, *The thumb slides back like so. It is what the Americans call a neat trick. Simple, eh?* And he was smiling. Her Fortuny.

And Lucy remembered, with startling vividness, the day, the hour, the moment when those words had been quietly uttered, when the manoeuvre had been demonstrated and the first of Fortuny's little tricks had slipped into her possession. She remembered that moment of illumination, recalled the marvel, the simplicity of it all. She rose from her chair and brushed the tuning keys of the cello with her fingers as she passed, unintentionally hitting the strings as she did so. A low discord, almost like a belch, erupted from the instrument then died. Suddenly she knew she had to get out, find space to breathe, make contact with this world, not with the memories of another. She grabbed a coat and ran down the stairs and out the front door.

The narrow streets behind San Michel were shiny from the evening's rain. The lingering car fumes had been washed away, the rubbish swept along the gutters and into the drains. The air was clean and tangy, almost tasted of rain, heavy and cool enough to drink. As she walked, she passed through warm pockets of restaurant smells—garlic, Asian spices, Greek kebabs, the sweet vanilla of crepes and the astringent aromas of wine and *Gauloises* from the Tabac bars. Lucy drank in her surroundings, so different from the dazzling stage set that was Venice, but even as she hugged the Parisian atmosphere to herself, plugged herself into the people and cafés and buzz around her, her thoughts returned to Fortuny, but this time with calmness and the clarity of understanding.

Fortuny, she now realised, had played for another age, and as much as she'd wanted to make that age her own, it wasn't. As much as she'd felt herself born into the wrong place and the wrong time, she wasn't. Fortuny's had been the age of dark, remote, all-seeing figures, more attuned to the age than the age itself, a whole dead mythology that she'd absorbed without even knowing, like the fairy-tales of her childhood. But he was gone now, and her own age was just out there, waiting to be interpreted. The gods, those all-seeing figures who breathed only the most rarefied air and whom she'd so longed to believe in, had departed. For once you'd supped with the gods, heard them speak in strange tongues, and then seen them moon over you and disintegrate in front of you because you didn't believe in them any more, they had no choice but to depart. And it was the saddest of sights, to watch the thing go that you once couldn't live without.

They went, yes, but not before bestowing the gift of their tricks on those lucky enough to receive them. Silently, she thanked Fortuny once again, but in such a way as to suggest that she would find her own path. And she imagined that she could even see his nod, the nod that everybody had looked for and few ever received. Yes, his gifts were in safe hands now. She would take them, the gifts of his secrets and little tricks, and do exactly what he would always have intended her to do: she would *use* them. Anything else would be a betrayal, for only in this way would Fortuny always be discernible through Lucy and, together, they would live on. Old father, she quietly mouthed to herself, old father, I leave you now, but I take you with me. You depart, you are here. I am weightless, come weigh me down.

Past and present. She swayed to and fro, to and fro. But as much as she wavered on the edge between the two, she knew that her age *was* out there, just as she knew, beyond doubt, that whatever Fortuny might have achieved in life, he would have nodded to her now, signalling that his gifts were in safe hands, and envying Lucy right now, standing at the lights, with all of it in front of her.

Read all about it...

MORE ABOUT THIS BOOK

MORE ABOUT THE AUTHOR

WE RECOMMEND

MIRA

Read all about it...

QUESTIONS FOR YOUR READING GROUP

1. Does Lucy fall in love with the man or the myth of the artist?

2. What is the enduring power of the myth of the Romantic artist?

3. Is it that art becomes a kind of religious substitute and the artist a kind of demi-god?

4. By the end of the book the myth has lost its power for Lucy. Why?

5. Is Lucy emblematic of the post-modern impulse to dismantle the whole Romantic notion of the artist?

6. Is she also emblematic of the reality that there are no neat divisions in history, that even though she imagines she is leaving one tradition behind, she is actually taking elements of it with her?

7. What does the book say about notions of the Old World and the New?

8. Are such notions still valid?

9. Lucy is twenty-three at the end of the novel – with "it all in front of her". What do you imagine will become of her?

10. Fortuny imagines himself to be a kind of Prufrock at the beginning of the book. How does the story echo TS Eliot's poem "The Love Song of J Alfred Prufrock"?

INSPIRATION

The book was initially prompted by a tale told to me by an Australian friend of mine who lived in Europe as a young woman. She was travelling through Italy one summer with a French friend. They were both sitting in a park in Rome one day when an elderly gentleman approached them and started to chat her friend up. He, it transpired, was a former concert pianist, she an aspiring artist. When he invited the young Frenchwoman – early twenties – back to his villa (he was clearly quite rich) she went with him. It was the beginning of a very intense, albeit brief, relationship. He was, my friend thought, short, squat and rather ugly. And whereas Fortuny is in his early sixties, this man was in his early eighties. Yet he exuded power, was redolent of the myth of the great artist (he was, apparently, well known in Italy) and this young woman believed in the whole idea of the god-gifted artist. He was also an aristocrat, a minor order, but I'm not sure which. As I thought about the tale (and it was, it seems, a summer-long affair) I started to wonder just what it was that attracted her, what it was that had such power over her.

Twilight in Venice is a speculation on this theme, that just as Lucy is seduced by the myth, the young woman, in the affair, was almost communing with myth made flesh in the form of this retired concert pianist. It can be read almost as an act of faith, something that is quasi-religious. The looks of the man, his age – none of that matters. It is what he represents. The more I thought about this, the more I started to wonder what would happen if this young woman were to *live* the myth to the extent that she dismantled it and in the process lost her

"... The looks of the man, his age – none of that matters..."

4

faith. So that, by the end of the story, we have a portrait of someone who sloughed off the very thing that has sustained her throughout most of her early years, and is forced to construct a new life, not based on inherited myth, but experience. In this respect, it is, at least to me, a very existentialist tale. It was also inevitable that notions of modernism and post-modernism would come into the tale (and post-modernism of course undercuts many of the assumptions crucial to both Romantic and modernist conceptions of art and the artist), but, at the same time, I wanted to avoid simplistic dualisms, because in life nothing is neat. There will always be over-lapping, even messiness. The actual affair that inspired the book was, by just about any measure, an extraordinary one. But not just because a young woman had an affair with an old man. It was the beliefs they held that gave the affair the extra dimension.

" …*Venice
itself is a kind
of living
museum…*"

VENICE

I first went to Venice in 1988 to take up a
residency at a writers' studio in Santa Croce. I
was there for two months, and through the
university (which administered the studio)
made Venetian friends that I have until this
day. I lived in a small flat just off the tourist
track and, surprisingly, many parts of Venice
are relatively free of crowds. Most people, it
seemed to me, stick to the main thoroughfares.
I've also lived in Canareggio and San Paolo –
where I wrote a lot of the early draft of what
was to become *Twilight in Venice*. Most of the
time I simply ate in, as Venice's restaurants can
be quite expensive. After a morning of writing I would often wander around the fruit and
vegetable market and then onto the fish market
– soaking up the atmosphere as much as buying
things. Later in the day I would run along the
Schiavoni and out along the gardens beyond
Castello. Often after a meal I caught up with
friends at many of the bars all over the city.

I probably haven't seen half the official must-see
sites. I prefer just strolling around and stumbling over places of interest. Venice itself is a
kind of living museum. But the Accademia
gallery – just for the Carpaccios – is really
rewarding.

MUSIC

I actually knew very little about classical music before starting this book. In fact, the whole book was very much a learning experience in music. I played in a pop band in the eighties, know guitar, and observed a few things about performers and performing. But my knowledge of the classics was abysmal.

First stop was Pablo Casals, the Bach suites for cello. It was almost worth writing the book just for the pleasure of discovering Casals. When I refer to earthy jabs of Fortuny's music, it comes from listening to Casals play Bach. Likewise Jacqueline du Pré – especially her rendition of Elgar. And, when I refer to Lucy sitting with her cello like a tradesman at his bench, it comes from watching du Pré at work.

Above all, though, my knowledge of music is very pop orientated – although I've branched out quite considerably since writing this book. Nonetheless, when Lucy hears Fortuny for the first time (and it is such a life-transforming event) it is, in fact, not unlike my experience of hearing The Beatles for the first time. My response was exactly the same as hers to hearing Fortuny – "That, I want to do that." And I did, for many years, until I realised I was a writer, not a musician. But the music that will always be special to me are the songs that struck a chord in that first Beatles album – songs such as "There's a Place" and "Please Please Me". Their power to transport never diminishes. It's not an uncommon observation, but it's one I'm happy to repeat, that, for a generation of writers growing up in the sixties, it wasn't the Great Tradition that turned us towards the artistic life – it was The Beatles.

BOOKS WHICH INSPIRED
Twilight in Venice

1. Quite a bit of Henry James, actually. Especially *The Aspern Papers*, a tight, brief (for James) novella of a young man ingratiating himself into the household of an elderly woman who has literary papers he desperately wants.

2. Jan Morris's *The Venetian Empire* is a brilliant study of the history of the empire and the city – which is rich in anecdote and tales.

3. Michael Dibdin's *Dead Lagoon* is a brilliant exploration of the underbelly of modern Italian and Venetian life. Containing, among other things, a lament for the decline of bribery.

4. A book of short stories by Italian writer Marta Morazzoni called *Girl in a Turban*. Wonderful, crisp style, and one story especially (about an aged musician, probably Mozart) caught my attention.

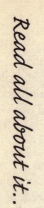

Read all about it…

AUTHOR BIOGRAPHY

I was born in Melbourne in 1949 and live in Melbourne with my partner and our son. I attended high school and La Trobe University where I eventually completed a degree in Literature and History. I taught in high schools and played in a rock band in the 1970s, usually about three to four nights a week in pubs (often "beer barns" that housed up to a thousand people) doing Eagles and Doobie Brothers covers. You can only take so much of that, so I left the band and formed my own doing original songs.

By then I decided I wanted to write – so I sold my Rickenbacher for an electric typewriter, packed my bag, and went and lived in a small French village just outside of Perpignan and wrote a play about TS Eliot, his first marriage and the writing of "The Waste Land", thinking that nobody would be interested in so specialist a topic. A year later – back in Melbourne – someone told me about a play called *Tom and Viv* which had just opened in the West End. The theatre company that had planned to do it dropped the play from the season – but ABC radio drama did produce it.

"…I eventually stopped writing plays, but kept writing novels…"

I eventually stopped writing plays and became a theatre critic but kept writing novels. I also taught fiction at RMIT in Melbourne and at Melbourne University. These days I write books, write book reviews for the Melbourne *Age*, jog, go to cricket training as much as possible and share in looking after my little boy. Writing – through residencies – has allowed me and us to live in different parts of the world – mostly Paris, Pont-Aven (Brittany) and Venice.

Read all about it...

Q & A ON WRITING

What do you love most about being a writer?

I don't have to go to work. Of course, writing is work. Often very hard, exacting work. But it's also a lot of fun. And I mean fun in a broad sense. Even with sad – or saddish – books such as *The Lovers' Room*, there is fun involved. I'm sure Proust – for all the seriousness of his project – was also having fun.

Where do you go for inspiration?

Books can come from reading other books or from life. But, really, there are no rules here – as there no rules for most of writing. Apparently Somerset Maugham once said that there are three golden rules to be observed when writing fiction – fortunately nobody remembers what they are. It should also be added that the whole notion of inspiration is over-rated. Most writers who go to a mountain top and sit around waiting for the thunderbolt of inspiration are still sitting there.

Where do your characters come from, and do they ever surprise you as they write?

There are no rules here either. They come from life, from books or a mixture of both. And I suppose they should surprise you. But I suspect because it takes so long to write a novel (two or three or four years) the characters evolve slowly over a long period of time. Almost incidentally. Or nonchalantly. At the end of the book you may very well look at them and wonder where on earth they came from. When, in fact, the prosaic truth probably is that they were slowly evolving the whole time. You were just too busy writing the book to notice.

"...Most writers who go to a mountain top and wait for inspiration are still sitting there..."

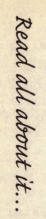

Read all about it…

"…writing is about production. Word production…"

When did you start writing?

I was a Johnny-come-lately to writing, after having very wisely misspent my youth in rock bands in the seventies. It was hard to sell my Rickenbacher (pretty much the same one John Lennon used) but it had to be done. I actually came to writing through painting, then music. First plays, then novels.

What one piece of advice would you give a writer wanting to start a career?

Write regularly – three or four sessions per week (each session about three or four hours) and aim to produce a thousand words a session. Do not waste too much time re-reading what you wrote the previous day – writing is about production. Word production. The very best you can come up with. That requires discipline and a clear head.

Read all about it...

A WRITER'S LIFE

Pen or Computer?
I always write the first draft by hand into a series of exercise books. It's not just an instant record of the work, but the act of putting pen to paper seems to connect me more with the story than going directly onto the screen. Possibly generational.

PC or Laptop?
I use a laptop – they go anywhere.

Music or Silence?
I never bother with music or anything like that, I just like a quiet place to write with no distractions.

Morning or Night?
I nearly always write in the mornings, usually from about 9.30 till about 12.30.

Coffee or Tea?
I rarely stop for any drinks – just go right through and get the most out of the morning session.

Your Guilty Reading Pleasure?
I can't think of any guilty reading. Besides, I write a non-fiction review column for the newspaper in Melbourne I contribute to and that takes a lot of time.

The First Book You Loved?
The first book I really read was Somerset Maugham's *The Razor's Edge*. It turned me into a reader, and I've read it many times since.

The Last Book You Read?
I'm two-thirds through Proust at the moment – wonderful writing.

Read all about it...

TOP TEN BOOKS

This is not in any order:

Marcel Proust, *Swann's Way*
Vladimir Nabokov, *Lolita*
Somerset Maugham, *The Razor's Edge*
George Eliot, *Middlemarch*
Alain Fournier, *Le Grand Meaulnes*
Graham Greene, *The Third Man* (novella and film script)
Tom Stoppard, Plays
George Johnston, *My Brother Jack*
TS Eliot, Poems
F Scott Fitzgerald, *The Great Gatsby*

A DAY IN THE LIFE

Very simple. I live in inner-city Melbourne. I have a small study in the back yard and after breakfast and after taking my son to school I go to my study and write for three to four hours. I usually aim for a thousand words a session. I have a regular non-fiction book column with the *Age* – a Melbourne broadsheet newspaper – and in the afternoons I try to get a review done. Afterwards, I'll go for a run, or off to cricket training and in the evenings, after a hard day's write, it's not uncommon to sit down at dinner with my partner, Fiona (also a writer), and share a bottle of bold Australian red.

"...I go to my study and write for three to four hours..."

If you enjoyed *Twilight in Venice,* we know you'll love...

The Lovers' Room by Steven Carroll

As the Allied forces occupy Japan at the end of World War II, an intense love affair develops between Australian Allen "Spin" Bowler, an interpreter in the British army, and Momoko, a woman whose calmness and dignity veil the tiredness and defeat she has suffered. In the quiet sanctuary of Momoko's room, Spin gradually sheds his shy bookish self and their love blossoms. However, the betrayal that follows has devastating consequences, forever changing the course of both their lives.

Everything Must Go by Elizabeth Flock

To those on the outside, the Powells are a happy family, but then a devastating accident destroys their fragile façade. When seven-year-old Henry is blamed for the tragedy, he tries desperately to make his parents happy again, but as he grows up, he questions if the guilt his parents have burdened him with has left him unable to escape his anguished family or their painful past...

The Butterfly House by Marcia Preston

Roberta and Cynthia are destined to be best friends forever. Unable to cope with her alcoholic mother, Roberta finds Cynthia's house the perfect carefree refuge. Cynthia's mother keeps beautiful butterflies and she's everything Roberta wishes her own mother could be. Years later, a stranger knocks on Roberta's door, forcing her to begin a journey back to childhood. But is she ready to know the truth about what happened on that tragic night ten years ago?

Read on for an exclusive extract of

The Lovers' Room
by Steven Carroll.

Available now from all good bookshops.

Prologue

Melbourne—June 1973

If he could have gone back and changed the order of the afternoon, he would have. Would never have gone out into the cold and the wind, would never have entered that wretched staff room, and he had regretted it from the moment he sat down on the soft black departmental chair. Even then he could have slipped out and nobody would have noticed. But he didn't, and chance, coincidence or just plain bad luck had done their work and nothing could change it now. If he were more of a superstitious person, he might even believe something like fate had called and he had answered. But, no, it was just rotten luck.

The garden light hovered like a full moon over the lawn, the black staff that supported it invisible in the gathering darkness. Allen Bowler, dressed in a tweed coat and brown felt hat, stood on the footpath, staring at the light, at his illuminated garden, his illuminated house, until the cold made him shiver. The street, opposite Melbourne University, where he had taught for most of his life, was empty. It was the shortest day of the year, dark by five. There were no other lights on in the rows of Victorian terraces except those in the corner milk bar, which glowed invitingly for the last of the day's custom.

He had just walked back from a staff meeting at the university to bid farewell to some old colleagues. A meeting that had dragged on into darkness. Allen Bowler, Professor of English, was an established figure at the university and was often invited to university functions. Generally the invitations went straight into the wastepaper bin, but this afternoon, out of a mixture of obligation and sheer restlessness, he had gone along and had sat in a stuffy staff room, listening to endless speeches, and anecdotes he'd heard once too often.

'Professor Bowler?'

The voice was as crisp as the air he now stood in. So much so that he could have sworn he could hear his name even now, as though somewhere out there, in the dead of winter darkness, he was being called. Unusually, he'd gone to his room after the meeting to gather some books, and had looked up from his desk to see a young Asian woman standing in his doorway. She seemed to have materialised from nowhere—he had no recollection of seeing her in the corridor, yet there she was, addressing him in the light, casual manner of an old acquaintance. The accent was English. London—he was a regular visitor to the city. The eyes, Japanese. Her face told you one thing, her voice another, and the disjunction of signs had been oddly disturbing. Indeed, he was grateful that he had been leaning forward, palms on the desk, and head down, reading over some old notes, when he'd looked up in response to the inquiry. It was a simple situation, he told himself afterwards. Mundane, even. No need to dwell, and he was a good dweller. A student had simply asked if he were Professor Bowler and he had looked up from his desk and nodded that he was. That was all. But there was nothing simple about the jumble of emotions he had felt then, and which he felt now.

The front gate squeaked open and he stepped in. It was ridiculous, but as much as he told himself he was not going to be held emotionally captive to some silly fancy of his, as he knew he was prone to do, the fact was that she'd stirred something in him that had lain dormant for a long time: she had stirred the young man buried inside the older man. And he'd have preferred things to have stayed the way they were, thank you very much, he reflected, slamming the gate behind him with sufficient force to sound a metallic clang through the otherwise quiet evening air. He should never have gone to the bloody meeting in the first place. But he had, and now his day was buggered—and for the most insignificant of reasons.

Annoyed with himself, he made his way along the narrow concrete path that ran beside his miniature garden, past the silver birch, the kumquat tree, pruned and shapely, the Japanese maples, the azaleas of the rock garden and the low ferns whose fronds shone under the garden light. As he mounted the steps that led to his front door, he stopped and idly scanned the garden. It was always a satisfying moment, the tranquillity of the garden acting like a natural balm whenever he returned troubled about something. And the house, too, was a sanctuary, closing the front door tantamount to locking the world out. But tonight the greeting of the young woman still echoed in his ears, the garden's calming powers were wanting and he was aware of something or someone following him in off the street, entering with him and violating the sanctuary of the house. The young woman, the face, the voice. That, and all the little things he couldn't even begin to put a finger on, disturbed him the way a sudden gust can disturb a pile of neatly raked leaves and toss them into the air.

Suddenly he was a young man again, and all the dreadful insecurity of the young man he once was came rushing back to claim him. The snapshots of his memory were thrown up from that neatly raked pile of memories he'd long ago hidden in some distant corner of his mind where they wouldn't be disturbed. And, thrown up, too, in this general disturbance, the name by which he'd once been known and which he hadn't heard in over twenty years: *Spin*. He dwelt on the sound of it, both strange and all too familiar. Then he whispered it softly to himself as he stood on his doorstep, as if, indeed, he were greeting the ghost of his former self. *Spin? Is it you? Are you back?* The question was spoken as if it were addressed to a past that belonged not just to another self, but to another body, another man altogether, who had lived another life that he knew about in the same way that he knew the lives of characters in books. As though this, indeed, were the figure that had followed him in from the street. Uninvited, yet with an air that it had every right to be there. But it wasn't someone else. This 'Spin' belonged to him— *was* once him—and the effect of speaking his old name again, however softly, was immediate, its power undiminished by time. As he paused, fumbling with his house keys, he was suddenly quiet, jolly, incidental Spin again. Nature's gentleman. Such was the absurd power of the word. That, and everything else that had followed and which came in its train.

Once inside, he took off his overcoat and placed his fedora on the hall stand alongside an impressive selection of other hats—borsalinos, Stetsons and the peaked sports cap he wore at the races. The stand was oak, its dark grains and knots gleaming from years of regular polishing.

He had been engaged to be married soon after the war, but had ended the engagement only weeks before the wedding date. The act shocked both sides of the family and still divided those who spoke to him and those who never forgave him.

There were no mementoes of the engagement in the house: no photographs, no letters, no candles from the cake carefully wrapped in tissue and waiting to be rediscovered one rainy Sunday afternoon. All that remained of the engagement was the hall stand. They had found it one Saturday morning in a second-hand furniture-and-book shop.

Since then there had been a long succession of what he still referred to as girlfriends, even though it felt odd to be talking like that at sixty—his birthday, the previous month, had been a quiet affair in a local eatery. But he was always being told he was the Peter Pan of the university staff, appearing to his colleagues to live an emotional life that belonged to another time. The jar of pills in the medicine cabinet for the faulty valve in his faulty heart, however—which only he and his doctor knew about—proved the contrary: that Peter Pan does not live for ever and looks can, indeed, deceive. His current companion was a lecturer in Shakespearean studies, but she was now living in Brussels and they rarely saw each other, except on trips, one of which—his long-awaited sabbatical—was coming up in a few weeks.

Allen Bowler draped his scarf across his overcoat, glanced in the hall-stand mirror, smoothed his hair and stepped into the study. He was a man who read. Everything. Or at least he used to. These days he seemed to flick through books more than anything else. His passion for reading was once such that he could sit for hours on end in his favourite armchair and barely move apart from his fingers turning the pages and his eyes following the print. Some of his most deeply satisfying memories were of reading when his passion for it was at its peak. As a student he had consumed *Anna Karenina* and *Middlemarch,* one after the other, without stopping for meals or even sleep, or so it seemed in recollection. But the passion had gone and he was more of a browser than a reader now.

All the same, the study was where he lived and its walls were lined with books: volumes on the Oriental languages that he once studied and the literature he eventually came to teach. The works of Matthew Arnold, J. S. Mill, Austen, Eliot, James and Conrad were prominent on the shelves, along with a section devoted to an almost complete set of *Scrutiny.* At Cambridge he had attended lectures given by Leavis, and *Scrutiny* was a legacy from that time. Following the Leavis lectures, along with other enthusiastic young students, he often attended afternoon teas at the luminary's house. Many of the old hard-backed volumes, early paperbacks and autographed first editions dated from that time. Underneath the set of *Scrutiny* were rows of other journals collected over the years, and manila folders filled with newspaper clippings as well as correspondence he had conducted with the authors.

He poured himself a whisky and settled down in his padded leather armchair. The shelves contained the gift of literature, the solace of poetry. The right works that, read in the right way, could nudge the world into greater tolerance. Bowler had taught literature for most of his life and had come to believe in it at a time when there was nothing else to believe in; not religion or country or politics, or any of the other discredited faiths. And he had clung to his faith with the quiet desperation of someone who dared not look back on his past or test his convictions too closely. Throughout the rainy Monday tutorials, the repeated lectures and the dull departmental meetings, he told himself again and again that he was doing what he did best and that that was all there was to be done. At least, if he followed that simple philosophy, his life would not have been wasted.

Allen Bowler had arrived at Cambridge in the spring of 1937 and often joined his college friends when they played cricket, sometimes to look after the score book, but mostly to watch and chat. The company was always interesting, the cricket absorbing. He loved cricket. Not that he could play. He'd been laughed out of too many school matches to think otherwise. Perhaps because of this he loved the game all the more.

One day he had been standing on the boundary line, not watching the game but staring at the deep green of the oval, the correctness of the rolled pitch and the sun on the clubhouse where teacups and sandwiches had been set out for the change of innings. All the time he was idly tossing a cricket ball in the air, its seam revolving in flight, then falling back into his palm like Newton's apple. A fellow student who had been observing him suddenly called out, 'Hey! That's what we'll call you. Spin. Spin Bowler.'

There was general laughter along the boundary line and the name had stuck, become synonymous with those first few years at Cambridge. He had carried it with him into the education corps of the British army, when many of his fellow students suspended their studies to enlist. In 1942, after the bombing of Pearl Harbour and the fall of Singapore, somebody mentioned that Spin spoke Japanese and he was transferred to Intelligence, where he stayed throughout the war. The name was distasteful to him now, but, since he had very few friends or acquaintances who had survived those days, he rarely had the displeasure of hearing it, and certainly avoided remembering it. Until now.

If only he hadn't tried to escape that general, indefinable sense of restlessness by going to the staff meeting. He could have stayed home and passed the hours harmlessly enough in his study and might never have encountered the young woman. It had ruined his day, destroyed his equilibrium, for, with that encounter, with that rush of memory, had come the name. He poured another whisky from the decanter and saw the young woman again, standing in his doorway.

As he sipped his whisky, he lingered over her image, wondered again where on earth in the building she'd emerged from and played this odd encounter over again in his mind.

'Professor Bowler?'

He'd nodded, outwardly composed, but inwardly struggling to find even the simplest response, and so he left it to a nod and to silence, while he waited for her to go on. Her winter coat was open and she stood with one leg forward; while he waited for her to speak, he stared, suddenly hypnotised, as she shifted the weight of her body from one foot to the other. Dreamlike. As though everything out there beyond his doorway and his room had suddenly dissolved, the world was suddenly an extension of his mind and his mind was no longer his.

She had then given her name, which he had immediately forgotten, as he usually did with students. She was English—just visiting, she said. Chatty. Both oblivious of her effect, and yet fully aware of the measure of it: at once innocent, and all-knowing. Her eyes told him that. At least, her eyes told his instincts and his instincts had taken over. She hovered in the doorway, waiting to be invited in. He sat, reluctantly. And the more she spoke, for all the innocence of her inquiries, the more his mind took the counsel of his instincts and the more he was convinced that she was fully aware of this thing that was happening to him. But why? She had appeared at his door, uttered a handful of words, and he was suddenly thrown, stirred, tossed.

She was studying the depiction of colonialism in literature. They all were, he thought. She rattled off the title of her thesis, but he didn't so much forget it as simply never bother to register it in the first place. Besides, he was too busy trying to calculate her age: mid-twenties, not much more. She went on. It was increasingly the case now. Nobody studied writers any more. They studied things like colonies, and their depiction in literature. Colonies, she was saying, they're either shoved aside—turned into a footnote or a small-talk reference—like the bad side of a dream that the book doesn't really want to know about. Or, they *are* the bad dream from which a hero walks away, all the better, all the 'rounder', for the experience. What did he think? Even if his mind had been functioning properly, he still wouldn't have understood what she was talking about.

'Why don't you speak to someone a little younger? Someone who knows more about these things?' he'd finally said.

'Because they'd only agree with me. I want someone who won't.'

'An old fogey?'

'C'mon…' She grinned, as if to say, don't play the old fart with me because we both know you're not.

She mentioned Conrad. That was his field, wasn't it? At least, she was told it was. Spin nodded, vaguely aware of a thesis that he'd abandoned in mid-sentence years before and never returned to. And it was while he was wondering why, that she said she was only here for another few days and could they talk properly soon. And, before he knew it, they'd set a day and a time.

And then she was gone, floated away. His door was open, the corridor outside silent, no sound, not even the footsteps of the young woman departing. She had dematerialised as suddenly as she had appeared, but the effect of her presence remained; her skin, her cheeks, peachlike, had been near enough to touch if he had stood and reached out, and something told him that he could, for he had touched that skin before. He sighed deeply, feeling the sheer weight of his memories and suddenly he could see it all again, plain as day. Suddenly, he stepped back into it all, was in the midst of it; those days of overheated military offices with their sickly scent of bubble-gum, cigarettes and stewed coffee, along with the image of the windswept, desolate streets of a defeated Tokyo outside. That, and everything else. By which he meant Momoko. Momoko. And it was disturbing, or just bloody maddening, that even now, after another lifetime, he still couldn't bring himself to say her name straight out. Even silently to himself in the privacy of his study. The phrase 'That, and everything else' had first come to mind. Only then had he pronounced her name in his head, as he would have all those years ago, lingering on each syllable. Mo-mo-ko.

On a shelf in the corner of the study, almost hidden behind a vase, sat a Japanese doll dressed in what had once been a light-green kimono. Now, the thin material of the dress was faded and the amateurish dabs of paint that once coloured the face were almost completely gone, revealing the bare, beaten tin underneath. A matchstick umbrella rested across one shoulder and, although its rice paper had yellowed over the years, it was still intact. He imagined the young man who made the doll scurrying along footpaths and picking up matchsticks dropped by strolling GIs. He would have measured the success of his day by the number he found, along with the discarded tins, string and paper.

He picked up the doll, examined it from different angles, then turned it on its head. There was a metal lever underneath it and he wiped the dust from the mechanism. Constructed out of rubble, it was a marvel, a monument to its maker's ingenuity. Slowly, he turned the lever, completed two revolutions, then let it go. For ten seconds a sparse, single-string folk tune played in his hand and he was Spin again. He closed his eyes, feeling like a reformed alcoholic risking just one drink for old times' sake.

But the sudden image of a young woman with blood running down her chin intruded into the music. Her eyes stared directly at him, whether in reproach, pity or anger, he couldn't be sure. All that mattered was what the look said: *Now, you join the rest.*